"Andrew Gretes' debut novel, *How to Dispose of Dead Elephants*, is a richly imagined and vibrant piece of writing. Illuminating the irrefutable complexities of family and his protagonist's evolution into adulthood, Gretes manages to reveal memorable, multi-textured characters with stunning originality, humor and deep compassion, while addressing the many questions inherent in what it means to be human."

Denise Orenstein, author of
The Secret Twin and *Unseen Companion*

"Aesop's fables, Punic Wars, Delphic Inc., what world are we in and how did we get here? We're on a joyride with Stubb, Mark, and trickster grandfather Papou, in search of nothing less than the meaning of life. This inventive novel, filled with non-sequiturs and riddles, also offers nuggets of wisdom: humans are no better than yogurt, no worse than vinegar. Love doesn't come from the heart, but the bellybutton. If you have a taste for zaniness and wit, this novel's for you."

Barbara Goldberg, author of *The Royal Baker's Daughter*,
Marvelous Pursuits and *Cautionary Tales*

"Wonderful, delightful, wildly original, and funny. Gretes conjures up a fable all his own."

Murad Kalam, author of *Night Journey*

Andrew Gretes received his MFA in fiction from American University. He has published poetry and short stories in various literary journals, including *Fiction Fix* and *The Monarch Review.* He currently resides in Washington D.C. *How to Dispose of Dead Elephants* is his first novel.

HOW TO DISPOSE OF **DEAD ELEPHANTS**

Andrew Gretes

First published in Great Britain
and the USA in 2014 by
Sandstone Press Ltd
PO Box 5725
One High Street
Dingwall
Ross-shire
IV15 9WJ
Scotland.

www.sandstonepress.com

Commissioning Editor: Robert Davidson

The publisher acknowledges subsidy from Creative Scotland
towards publication of this volume.

ISBN: 978-1-908737-65-6
ISBNe: 978-1-908737-66-3

Cover design by Jason Anscomb
Typeset by Iolaire Typesetting, Newtonmore.
Printed and bound by Totem, Poland

For Mom and Dad, Yiayia and Papou

When everything has stalled,
When thought is immobilized,
When language is silent,
When explanation returns home . . .
Then there has to be a thunderstorm.

– Søren Kierkegaard

PART I

THE FOX AND THE GRAPES

CHAPTER 1

My father gave me an assignment when I was sixteen. He said, "Son, write an Aesop fable."

The request, to give my old man credit, was at least in keeping with his preferred style of parenting: educational non-sequiturs. The assignment resembled projects Dad had doled out in the past, like the time he inserted a straw in my glass of water, put his thumb on top of the straw, and then lifted the straw out of the water, allowing my nine year-old self to gawk at how the liquid within the straw defied gravity, only to hand me a physics textbook the following morning bookmarked on a page about "air-pressure" with a rhyming couplet scribbled in the margin:

Son, magic is a forgery;
Solve the science behind the sorcery.

Or the time he found Mark and I squabbling in the backyard and told us to stop what we were doing so we could help him in amassing a pile of sticks, a pile which he then bound with nylon rope and challenged us to snap in half. Not ones to shirk orders of destruction, my best friend and I tackled the task, taking turns to squeeze the bundle of sticks under our shins, maintaining our balance for as long as possible, pressing down with every ounce of our gangly middle school bodies, but failing, in the end, when push came to splinter. Untying the bundle, Dad then handed Mark and I one stick apiece. He renewed his challenge and watched as we not only snapped our respective branches with ease but set up, unwittingly, his punch-line: "The same is true of you two," he said, "together you stand; divided you break." It was a moral which was certainly impressive at the time but not entirely helpful in settling our debate over whether or not Mark's iguana, Septor the Surreptitious, was half-dragon on its mother's side.

The protagonist of my first Aesop fable was a pregnant mountain. When news spreads of the expecting crag, spectators gather from all over the world. Some predict the mountain will give birth to a golem of gold. Others a flying yak. Others a river of plenty. But after a labor of earthquakes and avalanches, the mountain gives birth to a mouse. The moral—*Refrain from expectations.*

My father, a closet Aesop scholar, detected the plagiarism immediately. Returning the fable to me, he complimented my literary embellishments and even noted a place in the text where a conjunctive adverb could provide the necessary ballast for a floating semicolon. He then adjusted his Buddy Holly glasses and amended his request: ". . . a *novel* Aesop fable."

My second draft was about a deranged wombat who couldn't understand why kangaroos were so popular outside of Australia. Incensed, the wombat purchases a .38 special and blows away an innocent joey. It then chops the baby kangaroo up, stuffs its corpse into a duffel bag, and buys a plane ticket to America. There, the wombat murders a baby deer, hacks it into pieces, and stuffs it inside the same duffel bag. It then purchases a bus ticket to New York City where it drags its luggage to the middle of Times Square and screams out at the top of its little rodent lungs, "Americans, behold! Kangaroos are nothing special after all: they're deer! They're Australian deer! Look—see for yourselves!" But in order to fit the two bodies into one duffel bag, the wombat was forced to mutilate its victims beyond all recognition, and so no human in the crowd is able to see the similarity the wombat is ranting about. Dejected, the small furry marsupial reaches into its pouch for spare change. It wants nothing more than to fly home and sulk over a foaming pint of Foster's. But the wombat is broke. The moral—*Envy is expensive.*

My father, one eyebrow cocked, scanned the gratuitous tale in obvious disapproval. Having walked out of the theater during a showing of Monty Python's *Life of Brian*, my father had established a precise threshold for zaniness. Not surprisingly, demented wombats hacking up baby kangaroos in an attempt to expose their pedestrian essence was beyond this threshold. Running a hand through his metallic-gray hair, Dad asked for a third fable.

The last draft was more personal, biographical. I titled it "If Aesop Wrote a Fable about Temporal Lobe Epilepsy." It concerned a young silkworm who, having completed a week-long binge of munching mulberry leaves, sets out to spin a cocoon. Once the worm is finished with spinning its cocoon, it closes its eyes, yawns, and falls asleep, dreaming of wings and wanderlust. But that night, a farmer discovers the silkworm and plucks its cocoon from the tree. The farmer carries the silkworm home and throws it into a kettle of boiling water. There, the grub—separated from its cocoon—convulses, shrivels, and curls into a stub. The moral—*Some metamorphoses don't work out.*

My father abandoned the assignment shortly afterwards. No grammatical corrections. No synonym suggestions. No syntax manipulations. Just a half-smile on his lips. A wry armistice.

Four years later, here I am, waking up as if injected with amphetamines, an inexplicable urge to recover those old recycled Aesop assignments gushing through my bloodstream. What I don't understand is why I bolted for the closet at three o'clock in the morning in search of the original copies of those fables. Or why, upon salvaging them, I've spent the last few hours lying down in my attic bedroom, drowning all three in black ink, doodling Aesop vignettes into their margins—wolves devouring lambs, weasels enslaving mice, storks tyrannizing frogs, lions duping donkeys. Or why, on the last of these fables, I've drawn an old rockstar in a wheelchair who's wearing a Jolly Roger bandanna and smashing an electric bouzouki against the moral.

CHAPTER 2

Our swing-set looks like it's been sacked by Caesar. The vertical beams are scarred and splintered. The horizontal beam is graffitied—the words "Veni, Vidi, Vici." carved into the wood.

Three of us swing: Papou, Mark, and I.

Papou's wearing his Jolly Roger bandanna—the one I drew on his forehead last night. Eyes electric-blue, hair blizzard-white, my grandfather sits in the middle swing and shakes, rocking to the rhythm of a palpitating pendulum. The old man's face has solidified into a Parkinson's mask. In response, he's become a disciple of deadpan. Take last week for example—I was on an errand to retrieve one of Yiayia's romance novels from my grandparents' bedroom when Papou rolled up behind me and said, "The sky is my roof, the earth is my basement, but this room's my underwear—what are *you* doing in my underwear?" The old man's face was as expressionless as a manikin. Unlike his heart, Papou's face never breaks character. Recently, he's begun slipping Buster Keaton and Charlie Chaplin films into the VHS player, channeling his childhood adoration of silent comedy into an autumn vocation, preparing for obstacles to come: vocal speed-bumps down Parkinson Street.

Mark rocks his seat higher than he should. His hair is black bangs and alfalfas, his face pockmarks and cheekbones. Clothed in a crimson tunic and homemade sandals, my best friend is a "before the common-era crossdresser," a member of a historic role-playing organization known as the SCA, the Society of Creative Anachronisms. On the weekends, Mark travels to various campgrounds around the Eastern seaboard, donning his alternate persona: Marcus Cornelius Scipio Asianus, a fictional Roman foundling who was adopted into one of the most celebrated families of antiquity.

On weekdays, Mark dons his default persona: my best friend, a Korean adoptee and Starbucks barista who, at the age of three, was pumped full of vitamins by Catholic missionaries and shipped to the relatively obscure family of Ed and Martha Connor. Mark's birth—2,000 years belated, 5,000 miles afoul. Since graduating high school, his fascination with the SCA has burgeoned from a hobby to an occupation. Mark's second source of income is selling swords to a fictional world.

I sit in the left swing, absorbed in our backyard view: scattered maple trees and the yellow dome of St. Helen's Greek Orthodox Church. It was there, inside that golden skullcap, that I first learned such valuable life lessons such as never to agree to listen to an hour-long theological chant in medieval Greek in exchange for anything—not even something as delectable as the custard-stuffed goodness of *galaktoboureko*. Or, on a more positive note, that Saint George, my ancestors' patron saint, was by far the coolest saint in the church's canon, having slew a dragon, rescued a maiden, and decontaminated a water hole, and all in one fell chivalric swoop. Having recently dropped out of college, I'm one of those 20 year-old sons who indefinitely occupies his parents' attic. My head is brown curly hair and white dimple scars. Picture Humpty Dumpty circa 183 AF—after the 183rd fall.

Mark asks Papou what happens after death.

The question might appear random at first. But this, this is a tradition of ours: Mark and I swinging on both sides of Papou, the old guru fielding questions on death, life, and limbo—recess giving rise to the meaning of life.

Rolling his head in infinite circles, Papou responds, "Boys, not to fear. The afterlife is Halloween. If you've been good, you're given free rein by the old rabble-rouser upstairs to knock on the doors of the living and trick-or-treat."

My seat is warped. In middle school, the equation *me jumping on my wooden swing = Hannibal riding his war elephant* seemed rational. Each of the ropes to Mark's swing bears a scar, a knot. I severed the left rope the summer he went to "Adoptee Camp," my act inspired by a lonely voodoo-doll sort of mentality. We severed the right rope together—for symmetry's sake. Papou's seat is spotless. After he built the swing-set, he tested the middle one. It's been his ever since. Trespassers will have their asses severed.

As the sun continues to set, I continue to yawn, confirming my earlier suspicion that last night's jolt at three o'clock in the morning and the doodle debacle that ensued was not, as I had hoped, a dream. I want to ask my grandfather his thoughts on the matter. I want to ask Papou what he thinks it means to wake up suddenly as if resuscitated by a defibrillator manufactured by Thor. About what he thinks it means to jolt out of bed with a primordial urge to cat-scratch over morals. About what he thinks it means for his grandson to draw him smashing his Greek guitar against an imaginary stage like a coked-up rockstar . . .

But I inquire about apple-bobbing in the afterlife instead.

Papou assures us that bobbing for the fruit of the tree of good and evil is a common practice upstairs.

The ground at my feet bleeds a dark brown. It's a fresh wound in historic, swing-weary grass. If I were to dismount, dig with my fingernails, and become a backyard-archaeologist, I know what I'd find: broken wooden swords, cracked shields—fossils of empathetic inspiration. I used to rush home every day, eager to emulate my epileptic generals of antiquity: Alexander the Great, Julius Caesar, and Hannibal Barca.

Mark asks Papou if there's such a thing as "love at first sight."

"Love, maybe not . . ." the old man answers, "but there *is* such a thing as 'knocking-your-socks-off' at first sight. Anyone who says otherwise is a dunderhead." Papou wiggles his toes as his legs dangle from the swing. "As for love," he says, "that's more of a lunar thing. At first, everything is shrouded and new—crushes and crescent lips. Then, all of a sudden, everything splits in two—halves seeking other halves. Until finally, everything rounds out and becomes brighter than a star rigged with Christmas lights. Your full-love, boys, it just takes a little bit."

Despite the merit of the old man's answers, Mark and I continue our interrogation, alternating questions, tossing curveballs, urging the old trickster to perform once more: to transmogrify the gravity of Earth into a Martian moon-bounce.

I ask Papou if humans, by nature, are benevolent creatures.

The old man shuts his eyes. He furrows his brow and jiggles his head as if consulting a magic 8-ball within.

"No better than yogurt," he concludes.

Mark asks if humans are malevolent creatures.

"No worse than vinegar."

Anticipating further questions, Papou waves his hands in the air and elaborates: "Boys, when a man passes by a tavern and sees a tippler passed out on the street, what does he do? Does he steal the tippler's clothes and rummage through his pockets? No. Does he leave the tippler be and let the man rest in peace? No. So what does he do? Well, if he's a man, he collects as many friends as possible, gives them each a rundown on the situation, and places a crown on the tippler's head. He then wakes the bum up and pretends that the tippler's really a king and that he's only been dreaming he was a lifelong drunk, pestering the poor guy until he finally believes every word of the gag. Until, eventually, one of the actors breaks character, causing everyone else to do likewise in a fit of laughter. That's when the tippler realizes he's been had. That's human nature. Man's an imp, boys—no worse, no better."

The sun continues its descent, plummeting from an afternoon askew to an evening exodus. It's a welcome decline on a cloudless day in mid-July, a day capable of tempting even the most hardened of construction workers to sport a parasol.

I ask my grandfather if wisdom can be taught.

"Wisdom . . ." Papou muses. "It all depends on what you mean by that word, *Kalo Pathee.*"

The epithet *kalo pathee* is Greek for "good boy." It's what Papou's called me ever since I abandoned my birth name, Constantine, for my childhood nickname, Stubb. Having supplanted the emperor, I had, inadvertently, opened wide the gates to the barbarians of nomenclature, inviting in such stewards as my grandmother's

Kamari Mou, my boss' *Colilla*, Mark's *Killjoy*, Dad's *Son*, and Papou's *Kalo Pathee*.

Mark asks what Papou means by wisdom.

"I mean one's ability," the old man answers, inserting poignant dramatic pauses along the way, "to tell a story well. That's wisdom boys. Anyone who says otherwise is a dunderhead. Myself, I can say without a doubt that wisdom can be taught, for I've seen the miracle firsthand."

Fireflies begin to populate the summer air. They orbit us like incandescent satellites, chatting in the language of light.

"Now, *my* father," Papou continues, "was a horrendous storyteller. Remember that myth about the monster with a hundred eyes, the one where the hero has to tell the most boring story in all the world in order to lull all hundred eyes asleep. My father, he was that hero, and I, every night of my childhood, was that monster. So, one day, in self-defense, I set out to teach my father how to tell a story without slaying his audience . . ."

Papou gesticulates with each word, layering his story in the vernacular of mummery—that forgotten language which has the power to make even the most mono of linguists fluent in two languages. He recounts how, one fateful night, he interrupted his father in the middle of an especially soporific story and asked, "*Baba*, what's a story?" Papou's father, a reincarnation of the laconic Spartan warrior, pointed to the authentic library-blue binding of the book he was holding in his hands and then resumed his reading without further explanation. But Papou's five year-old self, a reincarnation of Socrates, inquired, "*Baba*, I don't understand—can you explain to me what a story is?" Glowering at the boy, the father replied, "A story is what I'm telling you right now—do you understand, *Moro*?" *Moro* being the Greek pet-name for "moron child." Minutes later, the boy, apparently not understanding, was at it again, causing his father to raise his voice in response, "*Moro!* A story is something which begins with 'once upon a time' and ends in 'ever after'!" But Papou, pushing his father's paternal fidelity to the limit, asked again, only to be answered this time by his father's frothing at the mouth, standing up, facing the lamp, and shadow-puppeting a dog with one hand and the moon with the other, producing an impromptu performance of the dog eating, vomiting, and then urinating on the moon. "That, that's a story!" he concluded. But Papou, feigning a potentially lethal-level of density, asked yet again concerning the nature of stories, forcing his father, who was unable now to hold his fury back any longer, to curse so loud that everyone in the house—Helen, Sophie, Nicky, Demo, and Vula—all rushed up to the attic in response and knocked on the door, concerned for the boy's life. It had only been a year since they had all immigrated to the States, each chipping in what they could to rent the upstairs of a Norfolk rowhouse, and it was this proximity which frightened the other members of the house so much, for each had heard the full sonic wrath of Papou's father, and so had rushed to inspect the old dragon's eyes for traces of infanticide. But finding the boy ostensibly alive and his father relatively composed, they left the boy to his fate, shrugging to themselves as they descended. Papou, intrepid, repeated his inquisitive refrain once more. This time, his father opened the attic window, grabbed his son by the arm, and dragged him out onto the roof, where the two stood silently for what seemed like eons to the boy—father and son, necks craned starward, eyes connecting the immortal dots above. And after they had climbed back inside the house and shut the window closed, the father gave an answer which had the startling result of satiating the boy: "That *Moro*, that is a story—it's something which propels you outside and forces your eyes to wander up. That's why each story begins with 'once upon'—what they're really saying is 'once *up* on'. Do you understand?" Papou, lying down again on his mattress with his hands folded under his pillow and his ears pricked wide, responded in delight, "I think so, but can you give me an example. *Baba*, can you tell me a story?"

"And it was the best story," Papou comments, his swing slowing to a tick-tock tremor, "my old man ever told. So, yes, boys, at some personal risk, wisdom can be taught."

A sapphire-blue tint envelops the sky. The shift is sudden,

supernatural, as if God had decided on a whim to inspect his creation below using a color slide.

"But to tell a story well," Papou says, "one has to first believe in the power of words. And no, not just their powers for good, but their powers for danger, for peril, for black magic. One must fear that if they say the word 'eclipse', there's a chance they might blot out the sun. One must think before using the word 'pit': *I might never climb out . . .*"

I picture a magician tying a bandanna over a volunteer's eyes. This, according to Papou, is a dangerous act. Having conjured the night, the magician must become light.

Docked to our left is Papou's wheelchair. His geriatric lifeboat. Any minute now, Mark and I will have to lift my grandfather up and return him aboard that fucking dinghy.

But I'm not going to think about that. I won't think about that. I'll heed Papou's advice instead. I'll harness my belief in the power of words. I'll repeat the number "1990" to myself like a time-machine mantra—"1990, 1990, 1990"—until I can pronounce the words just right, magically transforming today's date to a time in which neither Papou nor I had begun our shaking, a time when words like "Parkinson's" and "epilepsy" meant as little to us as remote cities in diametric hemispheres. The year, if I can just say the words correctly, will be 1990, and our movements will be our own, movements as smooth as a new mirror's skin—no distortions, no warps, no unnecessary bends—only reflections of what, once upon a time, had always been.

CHAPTER 3

Last night, I did it again. I couldn't help myself. After brushing my teeth, I felt an urge in my left hand. A spasmodic tingling. Before I knew it, I was holding a pen in my hand and scribbling on the metal surface of my desk, watching as my wrist twitched back and forth in a quarantined seizure, doodling little scenes from Aesop's fables: dolphins drowning monkeys, scorpions impaling toads, ants mocking grasshoppers, foxes exploiting goats—not to mention a scene which has nothing to do with Aesop's fables: Papou dressed in leather tassels and a Jolly Roger bandanna, shattering an electric bouzouki in wild abandon. When it was finally over, I rolled into bed and fell asleep, dreaming that my head was a castle, my neurons nobility. Leaning over the parapet of my skull, the prince sighed, "There's something rotten in the state of Stubb . . ."

"Killjoy? . . . Stubb?"

"What?"

"Just making sure you're awake."

Mark, he's dappled in sawdust, sitting cross-legged on the carpet of my bedroom, sanding a four-foot pole of wood. Technically, he's on the clock right now, working at making products for the SCA, weapons he hopes to sell to high school history teachers who moonlight on the weekends as Knights Templar. The vocation Mark should claim on his taxes: "blacksmith."

I ask Mark when my bedroom became his cubicle forge.

"Dude," he says, "you're killing me."

"I don't know what that means . . ."

Mark points to my dresser, where a glass of gin and tonic lies "wounded"—half-full. Mark says, "I've something profound to say, but I can't waste it on sober ears."

I sit up. I reach from my bed to the dresser and finish the drink.

"If you think about it," Mark says, spilling his promised profundity, "Jesus—the messiah of a billion or so people—is a zombie."

Earlier tonight, Mark climbed the stairs to my attic unannounced. Although he doesn't live here, my parents gave him a key to the front door the day we graduated from high school. Mark had been a staple of our lives for so many years that I was surprised he didn't already have one. Until recently, one of our neighbors was actually convinced that my parents were the ones who had adopted Mark from Korea eighteen years ago. But the truth is the inverse. Eighteen years ago, taken in by a family two streets down composed of an overworked mother, an older sister, and an aloof and now divorced father who recently moved to New Mexico, Mark adopted us.

After climbing the stairs to my attic bedroom, Mark declared, "The outside world sends its regards." He was toting a handle of gin, a zombie movie, and a pillowcase of SCA material. Standard Mark luggage.

For the past hour, Mark's zombie movie, *Lobotomies are Contagious,* has been playing on my bedroom TV. The film fluctuates from scene to scene, unable to make up its mind on whether it wants to pay homage to George Romero or Lucio Fulci—low-budget camp or macabre perversity. The film is set in London. Whenever a character is bitten by a zombie, they begin speaking in an American accent. That's how everyone else knows they're a lost cause.

Currently, two "Americans" are chasing a potential victim across the street. One of the zombies has tripped over its own legs and fallen face down in the middle of the road. The other zombie has halted temporarily, rotating its head from its fallen comrade to an approaching double-decker omnibus.

Mark grabs the remote. He pauses the movie. He quips, "What would Jesus do?"

I ask what happened to the beatitude celebrating decomposition.

Mark asks what a "beatitude" is.

"You know, blessed are the meek, blessed are the poor—"

"So, blessed are the decomposed?"

"Yeah."

"And the inept."

"And the lurchers. Don't forget about lurching."

"I was getting there—Christ."

"Don't take the Zombie's name in vain."

We're probably going to hell.

Then again, I've known a prankster my entire life, my grandfather, who deserves neither heaven nor hell and therefore, as far as I'm concerned, disproves the exclusivity of those poles—a man not unlike the original Jack O' Lantern: that old Irish farmer who tricked the devil into banishing him from hell but who's trickery barred him from the pearly gates above, and who was then forced to light a pumpkin in the dark and set off alone in search of a final resting place, a third option for sidewinder souls.

Mark, a wooden pole across his lap, leafs through various sheets of sandpaper. He examines each one like a blind man, rubbing his hands over their surface, groping for the perfect grit-count.

Mark asks if I was bitten by mosquitoes yesterday while swinging with Papou.

"Not really," I say.

He shoves his foot in my face. It looks like a slice of pepperoni pizza.

"That's what you get for wearing sandals," I say.

"What's wrong with sandals?"

"They're like the mosquito equivalent to full-frontal nudity."

"So . . . these are hickies?"

"Herpes."

"Fuck you. Weren't you wearing shorts?"

"Shorts are like mosquito cleavage. They're nice and all, but they're no full-frontal nudity."

"Or maybe you weren't bitten because the mosquitoes were disgusted by your hairy Greek legs?"

"Dude, when you go bald, you're going to wish you had this much hair on your legs, so you can pay someone to graft it on your head."

"First, I'm not going bald. Second, that's just gross."

"What's gross is what they use if you *don't* have hairy Greek legs."

"Dude . . ."

The zombie who tripped in the middle of the road is now, thanks to the speeding omnibus, zombie roadkill. The scene is pathetic, full of pathos. Red spittle dribbling down its lips, the zombie, a quadriplegic, plays its own ruptured trachea like a demonic harmonica.

I turn to face Mark. I make a confession. I tell him about last night, about the Aesop doodling, about my father's old fable assignment, about Dad's reception—his Mona Lisa smile—about my three Aesop drafts: the pregnant mountain, the deranged wombat, and the boiled silkworm . . .

I ask Mark if he thinks any of it means anything.

Mark stares at me the way one stares at someone who's just claimed that cheese does not exist.

"Of course it fucking means something," he says. "What's wrong with you?"

"Okay, so what does it mean?"

"Were you bitten recently?"

"Bitten?"

"Yeah, you know, not by mosquitoes, but by like an animal."

"An animal?"

"Yeah, like a tortoise or a hare?"

"That's retarded."

"Killjoy, this is serious. You could have rabies."

"Aesop rabies?"

"Yeah."

"Or . . ."

"Or . . . there could be a boring answer to all of this."

"Such as?"

"I don't know. Maybe you just need to write another fable.

Except, this time, write one which is less dejected, less deflated. Less *you*."

"So all I have to do is write a peppy fable and these doodle spasms will go away?"

"Sure, why not?"

"Somehow, that's less retarded."

"But that doesn't explain your dad's smile . . ."

"No."

"You might have to show him your fable when you finish."

"What if I don't want to?"

"The Aesop rabies doesn't care what you want—"

"Can we please not call it 'the Aesop rabies'?"

"That's like saying can we please not call blue 'blue'."

"No it's not—"

"The Aesop rabies is clouding your judgment."

"Look, what if we call it 'Aesopitis'?"

"Impossible."

"Why?"

"It doesn't roll off the tongue."

"And 'Aesop rabies' does?"

"Now you're getting it."

Mark runs a hand through his hair, releasing a cloud of wooden dandruff. He refills his blue plastic cup with gin. He says, "But why in the world is Papou showing up in your doodles? What's up with that?"

"No clue."

"None?"

"No."

"Okay, I'll consult an oracle in Maryland."

"Yeah, I hear Maryland's good for that . . ."

"Seriously," Mark says, "I'm going to Hagerstown for an SCA event tomorrow. There's a hydromancer in that kingdom. He's legit."

I start to ask Mark what a "hydromancer" is, but then I stop myself and roll over, letting my spine sink into the mattress, folding my hands under my head as I stare into the attic sky. The ceiling is mahogany. Wavy lines. Warped blemishes. Rings saturated in time. Like the rings under the eyes of Father Time.

Mark's suggestion, it's not exactly earth-shattering. This is the same guy who convinced me when we were younger that the only authentic way to solve an argument was through aerial auspices. Pointing to the sky, he would say, "If I'm right, a flock of ducks will fly from the north into that quadrant." To which I would counter with a different prediction, perhaps geese wearing sunglasses from the west. To be fair, it was an effective method of solving arguments. Time after time, Mark and I were forced to agree that we had no idea what the hell we were talking about.

Mark shoves his wooden pole and sandpaper sheets back into his red pillowcase. He takes another sip of gin. He asks what I'm thinking about.

"The darkness of dirt."

"That's what I thought."

"That's why I said it."

"Killjoy, all serious thought is a prejudice."

"Is that what Jesus said?"

"Yeah, something like that."

"If thy gloomy brain offends thee, pluck it out."

"There you go . . ."

"What's happening in Hagerstown tomorrow?"

"You're missing the movie."

I roll over and face the TV. I ask Mark again about Hagerstown.

"We're reenacting the battle of Pharsalus. Caesar versus Pompey. You would like it. You should come."

"Where's Hagerstown?"

"Northern Maryland."

"I can't."

"Why?"

"I'm working."

"Call out sick."

"I can't."

And I know, to Mark, my answer is an excuse. A premature

conclusion reached before consulting man's most prized faculty: his ability to omit. This is the same faculty which Mark has embraced as his life's motif. Omission permeates Mark's world—from his SCA existence, where he omits the ancient realities of slavery, poverty, chauvinism, hierarchy, and brutality—to his own humdrum existence, where he omits his lukewarm relationship to his adopted family, his nonexistent relationship to his unknown birth-parents, the fact that he has no idea who he is, the fact that I dropped out of college last year because my seizures had returned with a vengeance, the fact that he's never even considered matriculating, the fact that Papou, our collective north star, is expiring in front of our eyes.

And honestly, I don't know if this is an unhealthy thing for Mark to be doing or if he's on to something, if this is an idea which will preserve the species for centuries to come, if omission won't become, in the end, our greatest adaptation. Perhaps it really is the case that all we need from life is a few drawers, closets, and carpets in which to tuck life's excesses into, bins in which to dispense with self-amputated appendages, shoots in which to toss surplus truths. And perhaps, if I thought harder on the matter, I'd realize how all of this relates back to zombies.

On TV, a small cadre of humans have taken shelter inside the British Museum. Some of the survivors are using Anglo-Saxon artifacts to ward off invading zombies. Others are desperately searching the Rosetta Stone for answers. Others are going into full panic mode, looting Assyrian tablets. Others, in a germane gesture, are walling themselves up in room 21, entombing themselves in one of the seven greatest places of all time to entomb oneself: the Mausoleum of Halicarnassus.

I give in and ask Mark what a "hydromancer" is.

He says he'll tell me if I go to Hagerstown tomorrow.

I call his bluff.

"They're people who solve problems by looking into water," he says.

"But what do they see?"

"Answers."

"Answers?"

Mark sighs. It's a recurrent sigh. Like a wisp of air warped by frequency into a boomerang of disappointment.

"You're right," he says, "you shouldn't come to Hagerstown tomorrow."

Tomorrow, Mark will return to his second life, dressing up in "period" garb as he bashes his opponents' brains in with wooden clubs swaddled in duct tape.

Tomorrow, I'll sit in southern Virginia with my boss, Jorge, as I work at a store called "The Closet of Comics." We'll kill time by inviting our customers to play games like *Werewolf the Apocalypse*, games which involve sitting in a circle, consulting character cards, and pretending to be werewolves who are fighting for the liberation of Mother Earth from her chief pollutant: mankind.

But tonight, we'll finish a British zombie flick.

The world has never lacked what Mark and I most need from it: nooks, attics, hideouts.

CHAPTER 4

I shouldn't have had that last gin and tonic. Alcohol is a seizure stimulant. I know that. Mark knows that. The Alexander the Great Lego figure in my hand knows that. My whole fucking room knows that.

By the end of the movie, the zombies had expanded to the shores of Scotland, where they prepared to set sail for Scandinavia, ushering in a new Viking Age. The film concluded with an avant-garde shot: a map of Europe—likened to a brain—lobotomized.

Before driving home, Mark promised "answers" from the hydromancer in Hagerstown—wanted or not.

It's a little after midnight. I'm sitting on the edge of my mattress, my feet firmly planted on the carpet, green bristles sprouting between my toes. If I'm going to have a fit, I want to have it now, before I fall asleep. Reflexes get short-wired after a seizure. If you have one while dreaming, you can roll over, suffocate.

When I was first diagnosed in the 6th grade, I used to have a fit every day. The majority of them were partial seizures: staring spells, rubbing of the hands, incessant swallowing, etc. Mom would perform vigils in anticipation of night fits. She'd hover over my bed, her shadow short and stocky, her gaze midnight-green. She'd pace back and forth—a genie corked inside her son's bottle. We'd talk about her job at the plant nursery, about budding and grafting, pruning and dormancy. I remember telling her during one of these vigils that the ancient Spartans exposed their imperfect children on mountain tops. She replied, "The Spartans weren't worth the powder to blow themselves to hell." I asked why. She said, "If they were, they would have realized that all adaptations begin as abnormalities."

In my left hand is a miniature replica of Alexander the Great. He wields a sword, a buckler, and a helmet with white plumes. The conqueror of the known-world is mounted on a brown plastic steed. The story goes that the horse Bucephalus was deemed untamable by Alexander's father. The king warned his son, "You have just as much of a chance putting a bridle on a centaur as on that horse." This was exactly what little Alexander needed to hear, for he was determined to conquer everything. Even horses. But I like to think there's something else to the story, some footnote which got smudged in the Middle Ages by fish oil and was thus forgotten. Maybe the boy secretly saw a kinship between himself and the horse, an affinity between the way his own limbs kicked and spasmed during a seizure and the way Bucephalus contorted and thrashed about. Maybe he thought to himself: "If I can turn this horse into Pegasus, what can't *I* be turned into?" Whatever the case, the boy set about examining the horse with the patience of an astronomer, noting, as the sun set, that what perturbed the horse was its own shadow. So he turned Bucephalus in the direction of the sun and confidently leapt on.

Spinning inside my CD player is an album called *Unknown Pleasures*. The band's name is Joy Division. The lead singer, Ian Curtis, was an epileptic who killed himself at the age of 23. Alexander and I, we've made it to the fifth track of the album, a song titled "Insight," in which Ian Curtis dictates the last will and testament of a strangled epiphany. The vocals were apparently recorded through a telephone wire—to capture the immediacy of distance. In some remote spider-corner of the afterlife, Ian, he's still performing, jerking his arms in stiff staccato, emoting his "dead fly" dance.

The first time I heard Joy Division was in the 7th grade. It was right after my neurologist had found my magic pill combination. For the first year, the drugs would work for a month or so and then lose their effectiveness—something Dr. Markham called "the honeymoon effect." I began to picture neurology as something murky, incomplete. Something like the stepson of Alchemy. A science of potions, cauldrons, and a goal, where no one had the foggiest notion which potions in which cauldrons attained that goal. Eventually, Dr. Markham and I settled on 400 mg of Lamictal and 200 mg of Topamax, and I went from having three to four seizures a month to roughly two seizures a year. And of those two, at least one of them was caused by not taking my medication. Either from neglect or rebellion.

Around the same time, Mom persuaded me to join an epilepsy support group. At first, I refused. Then I got defensive. Then I acquiesced.

When an unstoppable force meets a flimsy object, conflict collapses . . .

Besides, the epilepsy support group's schedule was finite.

There were seven of us altogether. There was the woman who wanted to be a mother but who was afraid her anti-convulsive medicine might damage her child's development and that she might miscarry because of a seizure. There was the middle-aged man with red hair who had to refrain from laughing because merriment triggered fits. There was the older man who had never had a tonic-clonic in his life—just spells, trances, déjà vu's. There was the woman who spent her days looking after her son, a kid who wore a permanent helmet, suffered from 40-50 seizures a day, and took about that many pills. The kid had stopped developing mentally and was going to be like that for the rest of his life. I made Mark swear that if it ever came to that, he'd put a bullet through my helmet. But the farthest Mark has ever bent on the issue is to say that he'll help me "fall on my sword." And then there was Derrick, the only other teenager in the group. His eyes were fortifications: round brown shields with black bosses in the middle. Derrick had sounded the retreat. He introduced me to Joy Division.

As a group, our conversations centered around anxiety, anticipation, weathering the lull between brainstorms. It was pointless to talk about the seizures themselves. For the most part, we didn't remember them. And what we remembered was ineffable. So we talked about our fears instead. We talked about our shadows. We talked about what it would be like if Alexander was to come and turn our heads in the direction of the sun.

On the wall adjacent to my bed is a poster: Raphael's *Transfiguration*. The top half of the picture depicts Jesus levitating atop a black mountain, his surroundings aflame in a cerulean supernova. If anything, he resembles a ghost, not a zombie. The bottom half depicts a shadowy herd of mortals, their hands pointing frantically in opposing directions. In the lower right hand corner is a boy having a fit. He's called "the lunatic boy." His right hand reaches for the sky, his left hand for the earth. He contorts like a scale needing weight from above.

I've always found an odd sort of comfort in the gospels. Where else is it so natural, even prosaic, to be sick? Leprosy, lameness, paralysis, palsy, possession—they're like biblical common colds. In the gospels, everyone wears their health on their sleeves.

Unknown Pleasures continues its descent down all ten doom-laden tracks. The music is minor chords. Cathartic despair. A procession through empty rooms and broken glass, describing people who lie in wait for themselves, people who remember nothing. The cover art depicts the squiggling pulse of a wayward star. A sonic snapshot of sequential radio waves. Judging from the album's macabre content, the star has long since imploded and mutated into a stellar Charybdis.

It's tempting to think of epilepsy in similar terms: as just one more transmitter from beyond—a remote sun radiating its waves to unwilling receivers. My first contact with this gyrating pulsar was in Mrs. Piper's class. The experience was memorable, awkward. Like a first kiss. My 6th grade Language-Arts teacher, Mrs. Piper, was busy reading from a post-apocalyptic novel. The main character of the novel was a young woman who had miraculously survived the outbreak of a deadly virus but who feared she was the only one left alive. Climbing a nearby mountain in order to quell these fears, she surveyed her surroundings with a pair of binoculars. And to her joy and terror, she discovered she wasn't alone. There was something else down there. But it was impossible to tell who or what. It was dressed from head to toe in a baggy yellow radiation suit. That's when the aura began. It felt good at first—relaxing, almost ethereal. Then I woke up on the floor—stiff, heavy, sore. I apologized because I thought I had fallen asleep. But everyone kept telling me I had shaken out of my desk and dropped to the floor, and that I had punched Mrs. Piper when she tried to cradle me. Mrs. Piper had a bloody nose. If the police had come and asked me to draw a picture of the culprit, I would have sketched a blob: a baggy yellow radiation suit.

I doodled again. My right arm's tattooed in black ink. Another fable fit. But this one was different—I was able to stay focused on the same story and draw the complete narrative of "The Tortoise and the Hare." I drew it in three panels, like an Aesop comic strip. But the tortoise I sketched is old. His shell has grown gray. I colored it in with pencil. Wrapped around the tortoise's forehead is a Jolly Roger bandanna.

Sometimes, when I'm waiting like this, I like to imagine what my guardian angel looks like. He's usually huffing, puffing, wearing a "God" jersey, holding his team's cap so it won't fly off. After careful consideration, I've decided that he's a benchwarmer and that his name is Clarence.

When the aura comes, I'll slide off my mattress and turn on my side.

If I'm going to have a seizure, it'll probably be a tonic-clonic. All or nothing. That seems to be the trend these days. Trigger-happy neurons. One misfire and, suddenly, there's a war.

If the brain is a boxing glove, the temporal lobe is the thumb, and the aura is five seconds before the bell rings.

I squeeze Alexander tighter, warning him of the enemy's arrival. The tip of his sword is broken.

Unknown Pleasures slips into a soft descending bass line. The drumming is mechanical, sterile. Ian describes how even losing control can become a routine.

CHAPTER 5

The guy who rode 37 elephants over the Alps, he's under my bed.

I'm dreaming.

The guy who's responsible for the single bloodiest day in ancient warfare, he's under my bed.

This sort of thing—Carthaginians pitching camp in the crevice between the carpet and my mattress—it's been known to happen after fits.

The guy who killed a quarter of the male population in Rome—

It's been known to happen after fits.

He describes how Italian housekeepers used to scare their children by saying, "Behave, or Hannibal will come and get you!"

It's been known to happen in dreams after fits.

He says, "Stubb, get up!"

My attic bedroom is dark, lit by the crepuscular glow of Newport News' suburban sky. An amber spotlight emanates from below, flickering under the bed.

I ask Hannibal what's wrong with his flashlight.

He says, "That's my eye, you idiot."

I ask if his eye is all right.

He says, "Only the dead don't blink."

Hannibal reaches out from under the bed. Various rings decorate his blood-stained fingers. He doesn't need to tell me that these are rings he's cut off the fingers of dead soldiers.

Like a waiter performing the old tablecloth trick, Hannibal strips off the cover of my mattress and then retracts his hand underneath the bed. He sniffs, growls, "You're twenty years-old and you still wet your bed . . ."

I grab my pillow. I scoot across my mattress until my back faces the wall, minimizing the space I occupy. I say, "I lose bladder control when I have a fit."

Hannibal slides his upper torso out from underneath the bed. His face is white scars, gray facial hair, and a single incandescent eye.

"When I had a fit at the battle of Cannae," he says, "I grabbed the soldier I was fighting and *shook* him to death." Hannibal traces a finger over his right eye—a calloused and sightless stump. "Stubb, every scar on your face is arbitrary. It's disgusting."

Armor clinking, knees popping, Hannibal slides out from underneath the bed and rises to his feet. Everything that falls under the general's gaze is illuminated, stripped of its hiding place.

"When I was a child," he continues "my father held me over a pit of fire and made me swear that I would never stop fighting the Romans. Embers tinging my hair, I screamed out our covenant. I never did—I never stopped fighting."

"I'm sorry," I say, "I'm not like you."

Hannibal throws his arms up in the air. His armor is caked in grime, as if the path from the 3rd century BC to my bedroom led through a series of sewers and aqueducts. Gnashing his teeth, he paces my room in zigzag disgust.

My father introduced me to Hannibal. Dad's response to his son's onset of epilepsy was to research inspirational figures in history who had not only survived but thrived with the disorder. Being a high school English teacher, Dad's plan was to use literary exemplars like Dostoevsky and Tennyson in order to instill in his son a chosen-one mentality. But knowing all too well that I had been bitten by the fantasy bug, Dad curbed his curriculum from the pen to the sword. I remember, when he first taught me that Hannibal had marched his elephants over the Alps, I wasn't struck so much by the chutzpah of the act but by its logic, its symmetry. I wondered what the big deal was. Was there an animal *more* suited to the immensity of mountains? The real absurdity, I thought, would have been if Hannibal had marched ponies over the Alps. I felt an immediate kinship to this misunderstood Carthaginian—if, for no other reason, than for the fact that other than spasming to the floor we also shared the experience of riding an elephant.

My own elephant ride happened when I was seven, on a day in which Yiayia and Papou took me to the zoo. Every summer, I was dropped off by my parents to my grandparents' house, where, after being sufficiently pampered and spoiled for a month, I was returned against my will. I remember feeling weird upon entering the zoo that day with my grandparents. The animals, they seemed like members of my extended family. There was Cousin Monkey, Nephew Eagle, Aunt Peacock, and Uncle Lion. And I guess, in a way, I was right. Man is the prodigal animal that never returned.

At the zoo, I rode an elephant named Cyprus. I still remember her name because there's a picture of us with a message scribbled on the back that reads: "Cyprus at your service—from tusk till dawn!" Later, when we were leaving, I asked Papou how all the animals ended up in the zoo. He said, "Orpheus brought them." I asked who Orpheus was. He said he was a musician whose music was so hypnotizing that everything followed him around like a magnet: stones, animals, humans, satyrs—you name it. I asked why he brought all the animals to the zoo. Papou said, "For money—what else?" "But what does Orpheus do with all the money?" "Gambles." I felt bad for the animals, and I didn't much like this Orpheus character. But I had to know more. I asked Papou what Orpheus did when he wasn't gambling. Papou said he took his winnings and bribed greedy zookeepers for their keys and then unlocked all the animals at night, unleashing them upon the city. I said, "That doesn't make any sense!" Papou said, "Of course it doesn't—who told you it made sense?" He explained that Orpheus was a musician and that nothing musicians do makes sense. In fact, the greater the musician, the less sense. It's the price for drinking of the river, Rhythm. If one wishes to play upon an instrument, one has to relinquish the reins and *become* an instrument. At the end of the day, the only thing under the musician's control is to remain in tune.

Hannibal ends his pacing. The light in his eye shifts from amber to crimson. Moving in for the kill, he lunges in my direction, grabbing my left leg and dragging me out of bed.

I reach for the mattress.

I reach for the dresser.

I reach for Alexander the Great.

Hannibal breaks open the skylight and climbs onto the roof, dragging me along like a log to the fire. Dangling my body off the shingles, he screams, "Swear to me!"

"What?! Swear what?!"

"Swear to me that you'll conquer the world! Swear that you'll sack the Vatican! Swear that you'll be the first to circumnavigate the globe with a hang-glider! Or just swear that you'll stop wetting your bed, for fuck's sake!"

Removed from the safety of my bedroom, suspended 20 feet high, I flap like a fish out of water, gills opening uselessly to the air of the outside world.

"Stubb, this isn't a joke—I *will* drop you . . ."

I twitch, smack my lips.

"Stubb, please . . ."

I soil my underwear.

When my head reaches a vermilion red, Hannibal relents, reels me in, and drops my body on the carpet. Chest heaving in brooding respiration, he stares at the stains on my carpet.

"When I have nightmares," he says, "I dream of a little boy who pretended to be me but who grows up to be a vegetable, a bed-wetter . . ."

I try to respond, but everything comes out gurgled. My body attempts to escape me through sweat, drool, snot, and urine.

"Stubb, stop haunting me. Never hide under my bed again . . ."

CHAPTER 6

Crouching behind a pavilion tent, peering through homemade eye-slits, my grandfather and I prepare to commit a tried-and-true ruse. The old man wears a black fez over his Jolly Roger bandanna—a gesture of traditional iconoclasm. Papou glides his left hand over various notes of his bouzouki's fretboard, while his right hand grips his wheelchair in restraint. Quaking in anticipation, he listens for the optimal moment to invade through the tent's back-flap. If the act of rolling on stage and challenging the musical libido of unsuspecting bouzouki players was a crime, my grandfather would've been injected with potassium chloride decades ago.

This afternoon, as Yiayia was heading out of the kitchen to visit some of her girlfriends at the Norfolk Greek festival, Papou rolled after her, his eyes pulsing with imprisoned energy. He declared that he and I were coming along. Having just returned from work myself, this was not only news to Yiayia but also news to me. I was hoping to climb upstairs and take a nap. It had been two days since the fit, but I was still having trouble sleeping because of all of this Aesop bullshit. Yiayia, knowing what her husband was up to, relented with the following stipulation: "If you get yourself killed, you're telling the children—not me . . ." In the car, Papou told me that marriage is about compromise.

"Look at Little Dimi," the old man whispers, his face pressed against the pavilion's canvas. "Kid closes his eyes when he sings. I bet he's picturing the crowd in their undies."

The outside air is infused with flavor. The smells are loud, pungent. They mingle and waft, propelled to innocent nostrils by an artificial breeze. The olfactory sirens of *pastitsio, moussaka, spanikopita,* and *doulmades* do their best to shipwreck local commuters to St. Sophia's parking lot.

I take a crumpled fez out of my pocket. The red hat is a relic of the collectively-dreaded experience known to all Greek-Americans as "Greek School." Once a week, for three years of my life, I was forced to sit in a classroom at St. Helen's with twenty other inmates and watch the Greek equivalent of *Sesame Street*, learning my 1's, 2's, and 3's not from a vampire named "The Count" but from a cult-leader, Pythagoras; being educated on the ways of misanthropy not from a garbage-dwelling grouch named "Oscar" but from a barrel-rolling cynic, Diogenes. Thankfully, when we got older, Mrs. Staboulos swapped the educational videos with soap operas, giving us the opportunity to bolster our Greek lexicon with such useful words as *kakos didymos,* "evil twin," and *sousourada,* "minx."

I hold up my fez, waving it in the air, secretly hoping some bird will swoop down and swipe it away. When that plan fails, I ask Papou if the fez is necessary.

He assures me it's pivotal.

When I try to protest, the old man just smiles and ignores me—far too absorbed in what's going on inside the tent. He watches the band as it plays through a set of Greek ditties.

The ruse which my grandmother was afraid her husband might get himself killed doing was originally invented in 1945 at the wedding reception of Papou's oldest cousin, George Marakas. Being a year out of practice with his bouzouki because of a stint in America's Pacific campaign, Papou was suspected of musical atrophy and snubbed of a position in a three-piece band for George's wedding, causing the old trickster—in keeping with the martial life he had recently been living—to smuggle his bouzouki inside the wedding, sneak up behind the usurper, and play the notes of whatever song his rival was playing a tempo above his opponent, challenging the musician's virtuosity in a duel of allegros, prestos, and, when push came to shove, prestissimos. As a result of this fateful day, no bouzouki player in southeast Virginia has been able to perform in a public setting since without shifting their eyes at least once in a paranoid search for imitators of the now famous maneuver known as "bouzouki blitzing."

Papou grabs my arm. His grip is wood-glue. He says, "I never play well when I'm not dancing. So you have to *make* me dance, understand?"

I nod. I swear that I won't fail the old man, that I won't impede his playing, that I'll act out the role of his surrogate legs like a thoroughbred thespian.

"Whatever you do," Papou warns, "avoid caution. Caution is the death of dance."

"I understand . . ."

"Did you remember the wine?"

I take out a bottle from my backpack, which I stole from my parents' cupboard. I lie it down in the grass.

"And your caution?" Papou asks.

"What?"

"Your caution, *Kalo Pathee*—did you remember that?"

"No . . . I left it at home."

Papou claps his hands in approval, laughing as softly as he can.

The Marakas double helix is a peculiar edifice. Every generation or two, God slides out one of our nucleotides and creates a precarious unbalance—a necessity for dance.

Papou quickens, jolts. He turns to me and orders, "Now, now!"

I grab the old man's wheelchair and plow us through the tent's tailcoat. On stage, a guitar player, a tambourine player, an accordion player, and a bouzouki player all perform to a crowd of thirty or so onlookers. Papou strums his instrument, gliding his hands up and down the guitar's elongated fingerboard with reckless precision, prompting the crowd to shout "Blitz!" and "Yasas!" in impish encouragement. The band reacts accordingly, a mixture of surprise and excitement governing their demeanor as Little Dimi, a teenager and one-time pupil of the old trickster, increases his playing tempo, officially accepting the challenge of Papou's bouzouki blitz.

I plant the wine upright in the center of the stage. The bottle is a flag: it announces our claim on the spotlight. I take up Papou's wheelchair again and rock it a little bit to the left, a little bit to the right, a little bit up, a little bit down. I do whatever I can to make the old man's wheelchair dance.

The song is one of Papou's favorites—"*Oloi oi Rebetes tou Dounia*"—a song of the Rembetika tradition, the Greek blues, which is famous for celebrating drinking, gambling, and sex amongst the hashish dens of depression-era Greece. The composer of the song is a pioneer of Rembetika, Markos Vamvakaris—a hero of Papou's who was a miner, a porter, a butcher, and a musician.

Hands palpitating over his instrument, Papou licks his lips, rocks his hips, taps his feet, and bobs his head, transferring his Parkinson's into a Dionysian muse. I do the rest. I make us dance, shaking our bodies as I mime the thing I hate.

The audience lights up. What was formerly a benign crowd becomes a fervent mob.

I can feel myself rocking the wheelchair too much to one side, too much to the other. I want to tell Papou that I know all about this moment, that it's best that we turn back, that I think we should slow down and abort the ruse. But there's no way the old man would ever listen to such talk; besides, he's too busy fighting his own battle at the moment: his fingers competing with the lapping of his tremors.

I shut up and close my eyes. I try to harness my inner-Mark. I try to omit every association I have between flailing upright and crashing to the ground.

Mark, he hasn't been answering his cell phone. He never does when he's at an event. It would be "anachronistic." Not that driving a 1989 Honda Accord to attend the event *isn't*. But that's the beauty of omission.

My balance falters.

My fez falls off.

I capsize Papou into the grass and then tumble on top of him.

The band stops. The audience stops. They rush forward and circle us, their heads competing to assess the damage. Papou winces, coughs, smiles, grimaces. He lifts his left wrist off the crushed neck of his bouzouki, revealing a splintered rupture in the middle of the instrument's silver fretboard.

We ask Papou if he's all right, if anything's broken, if he needs medical assistance.

Grabbing my arm, he says, "Never fear, we two, we have the advantage of having already been broken."

The tambourine player helps me up. The accordion player and Little Dimi hoist the old trickster back into his chair. Papou diffuses the moment brilliantly, like a veteran tumbler. He strikes up conversations about Rembetika, Markos Vamvakaris, and the legacy of bouzouki blitzing. He hands Little Dimi the bottle of wine in reconciliation and says that next time he'll be taking lessons from him. When the excitement of the incident winds down, Papou and I fade into the background. We listen to two more songs and make a relatively modest exit.

Rolling Papou in the direction of the church, the neck of his cracked bouzouki sticking out of my backpack like a sore thumb, I ask if he's sure he's all right, if anything's broken. I say, "I messed up. It was my fault."

"How else," Papou asks, holding his left wrist in pain, "could we have stopped?"

"I don't know. The way normal people do. At the end of a song."

"No," Papou says, "we didn't start with anything clean. Dance is messy. Do you understand? We can only work with what we're given. But what is dance?"

"Messy . . ."

"It's why we're such good dancers, *Kalo Pathee*. We're used to messy."

Papou and I brush past various tables. Vendors selling jewelry. Vendors selling rugs. Vendors selling language textbooks. Vendors selling *loukoumades*—balls of dough dripping in honey. But we put on our blinders and head straight for the parking lot, planning to hide the evidence of the accident before Yiayia ever notices.

Yesterday, I bought a notepad—the kind reporters use in film-noir movies. Now, whenever I feel the implacable urge to doodle

Aesop animals, I can do so on a pad of paper like a normal human being. I consider it a vomit bucket—but more portable and less conspicuous. I used it to draw the fable of "The Lion and the Mouse" at work today. It's the most elaborate fable I've penned yet. The first panel depicts a mouse accidentally stepping on a lion's paw. The second panel shows the lion, roused, inspecting its tiny prisoner. The third: the lion patting the mouse on the head and letting it go. The fourth: the lion snared in a hunter's net, helpless, roaring. The fifth: the mouse gnawing a hole in the hunter's net and freeing the lion. The sixth: the lion strolling in a sunny background with the mouse riding on its head, basking in brotherhood. When I finished, I thought of Hannibal. I thought of my most recent fit. Here I was using him to deal with my condition, impersonating him, imagining him, being him, but what had Hannibal gained in return? What cities had I sacked?

I open the door to my grandparents' car. The inside of the car smells like peppermint and old newspapers. We pop the trunk open and do our best to hide Papou's broken bouzouki under a pile of dirty oil rags.

When I purchased my detective notepad, I went ahead and bought a copy of *Aesop's Fables* while I was at it. I figured if I was going to write a new fable, I should start getting some ideas. Originally, I thought about borrowing Dad's copy, but the problem with that is that he'd notice. A hole in one of my father's bookshelves is like a hole in the wall. It's not that he'd demand that I give the book back or anything like that; it's that he'd ask me what I was up to. And I don't know the answer to that question. Besides, the copy I purchased has an appendix of Aesop's life, which I don't think his copy has. After reading the first paragraph, I was pleasantly surprised. It turns out that Aesop is my kind of guy . . .

> *Aesop was a slave, extremely ugly, filthy, snub-nosed, misshapen, dark-skinned, dwarfish, flat-footed, bandy-legged, short-armed, squint-eyed, and fat-lipped—in short, a freak of nature. What's more, he was unable to speak."*

After closing the trunk, Papou and I head for the church in search of Yiayia. Typically, my grandmother is a fairly easy woman to spot thanks to her curly white beehive and purple outfits. But at Greek festivals, *yiayia's* abound, making curly white beehives and purple outfits as good as camouflage.

I ask Papou if he knows any fables.

"Fables . . ." he says, "you mean, like fairy tales?"

"No, not exactly. Fables, they have morals or messages at the end. Like the story of 'The Lion and the Mouse'."

Papou thinks for a minute, teeth gnawing his lips. He says, "Yes, I remember now—the story of how the mouse teaches the lion how to shave so he can stop scratching his wife's face . . ."

Even if my grandfather wanted to plagiarize, I don't think he could. Every story is now his. If I was to confess my predicament of needing to compose an original peppy fable, it would be like a match confessing to a star its need to be struck.

Papou asks if he's ever told me about the time he "ouzo-dropped" his father.

I shake my head.

He claps his hands, winces, and pantomimes with palpitating excitement. He says, "My brother Demo and I, we used to ouzo-drop people. All sorts of people. We'd slip into the family restaurant and pour ouzo everywhere it didn't belong. But this wasn't normal ouzo. No, it was special."

"What do you mean? What was it?"

"Demo and I, we found the concoction in the restaurant one day—hidden away, forgotten, a batch of moonshine which had been sitting in the closet since the days of Prohibition. And trust me, there was a whole shelf of this stuff. There were so many bottles that Demo and I thought we had stumbled upon an alcoholic's bomb shelter. The liquor had been aged to the point of no smell, no taste. All that remained was effect. We nicknamed it *Koptees*, 'The Cutter,' because it had the power to unbind—even knots best left uncut. But how could we resist? You can only imagine how entertaining it was to watch old coffee-drinking stiffs suddenly become sloppy, to watch soup-slurping saints suddenly become lechers!"

"But why would you ouzo-drop your father?"

"It was the day after our Uncle Manolis had passed away, my father's brother. For whatever reason, Demo and I, we thought it might be a good idea to ouzo-drop Dad, to ease the old dragon's heart. You see, *Baba*, he had never learned how to laugh. At best, he could shrug. But after who knows how many ouzo-drops, Dad became more solemn than ever. Our plan had backfired. Dad took Demo and I aside. His voice was December. He said that every time a family member died, they gathered their flesh and bones and settled in his heart. He grabbed his hair and said that always, always, always his ancestors were asking him, 'Did you tell your grandsons about me?! Did you tell Yannis?! What about Athena?!' He said that the older the ancestor was, the more rotten they became, the more desperate was their need to stay alive in their grandchildren's memory. Dad, he looked Demo and I in the face—I still remember that face—a pale needy face. He said, 'Boys, there's a leper colony in my heart. They want me to be Christ. But I can't. I'm not.' Then he broke down. And only Mama could make him stop."

"But what does it mean?" I ask. "The story—is it a fable, is there a moral?"

"A moral . . ." Papou muses. "Maybe, if you want there to be . . ."

"Well, what is it then?"

The old man cranes his neck back and eyes me over his shoulder. Rubbing the sides of his wheelchair, he says, "Even from those we love most, we want always to be free."

CHAPTER 7

Some fathers and sons play catch. Others go camping. Others watch Monday Night Football together. My father and I, our bond is neighborhood walks: we amble habitually.

"Anhedonia," Dad says, his gray hair escaping from his Redskins' baseball cap, "do you know what it means?"

"Something like the absence of pleasure?" I say.

"Good. But it's also the inability to feel pleasure."

To the chagrin of countless passerby, my father and I make very poor eavesdropping material. Dad's a vocabulary fiend. As a child, he would read the dictionary while his siblings watched *Zorro* on TV. When his brother John would swing a stick in homage of his favorite Spanish swashbuckler, my father would interrupt: "Zorro uses an epee; that stick is the thickness of a schlager."

"But you don't feel anhedonia, do you?" Dad asks, adjusting his thick-rimmed glasses.

"No, I don't think so . . ."

Despite the fact that school's been out on summer break for almost two months now, my father's dressed in his standard teaching attire: blue button-up shirt, khaki slacks, and white sneakers. The way to tell whether my old man's been to work or not is to analyze the condition of his clothes, not their content. If his shirt is unbuttoned, his sleeves rolled up, his chest pocket stuffed with a portable stapler, and his slacks bulging with whiteboard markers, it's safe to assume he's taught at Warwick High that day.

About once a month, when Dad's not grading English papers or coaching varsity soccer, we take a walk. The first time it happened,

I was in the 9th grade. I was browsing through my father's books—yellow pages and worn spines—when he caught me eyeing one of his favorites, *The Man Who Was Thursday*. Leaping from his chair like a trap waiting decades to be sprung, he announced, "Let's take a walk . . ."

Most of the bonds my father and I accumulate are quantifiable. When we watched the documentary *Cosmos* together, Dad would create viewing quizzes after each episode before going to bed. He would then hand me a quiz in the morning over breakfast. Chewing my Cinnamon Toast Crunch, I'd read . . .

If you were to travel at approximately 300,000 kilometers per second (i.e. the speed of light), what would you see?

- *a) everything zoomed in as if through a microscope*
- *b) blue*
- *c) nothing*
- *d) exactly what Han Solo and Chewbacca saw in the Millennium Falcon*

Except Dad's quizzes didn't include answers like "d." As far as I know, he's never been tempted by the devil of facetiousness.

We halt at an intersection and turn right. Our surroundings are Newport News suburbia. Each yard we pass is an invitation for voyeurism. Some are hard to resist, like the one with the various tricycles and water-guns littered about the lawn and the lone pterodactyl kite stuck in the tree. Others are more everyday, like the one with the half-open garage with a radio inside playing NPR. Others are nostalgic, plaintive, like the one with the rusted basketball hoop—drooping, obsolete. Nominally, Newport News is a city which should be famous for its cigarettes or its newspapers. But in reality, if Newport News is known for anything, it's shipbuilding. The name of my high school was Merrimack High. The mascot of our local community college: the Navigators.

St. Helen's dome looms in the horizon. No matter how far or how long our walks seem to go, they invariably gravitate into orbits around that gilded dome.

As the road inclines up a hill, Dad and I begin to move in slow motion.

Dad says, "This is my favorite part." He stops and looks behind us. He savors the moment. He says, "There's something perfect about the slope to this hill. It's just steep enough without being too steep."

Analyzing the sidewalk for apparent parabolic perfection, I ask Dad what the hell he's talking about.

Dad ignores my question until we reach the top of the hill. There, he places his hand on my shoulder and says, "I'll show you—turn around."

"What for?"

"So we can walk back downhill. So I can show you what's so perfect about the slope to this hill."

And I know this is all leading up to one of my father's pedagogical insights. The man has a knack for ushering the routine in the classroom, turning a task as ordinary as changing the oil in the car into a lecture about the first law of thermodynamics. But curious as to which lesson he has up his sleeve, I play along . . .

One of the side-effects of trying to prod your son into identifying with Alexander the Great is that it forces you into the role of Aristotle—"The Master of Those Who Know." As for my part, there was a time when I was more eager to identify with the persona. Like when I first became frightened of memory loss, of knowledge being ripped away by the electric gales of brainstorms. To combat this fear, I used my knowledge of Alexander's life as a catalyst. In a time when reading was a public affair, something one did out loud, Alexander possessed the distinction of being able to read to himself without moving his lips. So I made it my mission to possess a quaint distinction of my own, but one more relevant to my fears. I set about fortifying a prodigious memory, one even brainstorms couldn't penetrate. In particular, I latched on to a mnemonic device known as "The Roman Room System." The device involves taking a room which you know quite well and then mapping it out visually in your head until every wall and every inch is as palpable as possible. Then, once your imaginary room has become a mental reality, all you have to do in order to remember anything is to store it in your room. For example, if you wanted to memorize the fact that Eratosthenes was the first person to calculate the circumference of the earth, all you would have to do is put a globe on top of your mental dresser with a belt girdling its belly and an inscription at its base: "Air gets tossed in a sneeze"—or whatever other inscription that might help you pronounce Eratosthenes' name . . . Of course, if you do this enough, your mental room becomes cluttered, clogged. So you're forced to expand and build a house. And then, if you're ambitious, a city . . .

Dad and I start heading back down the hill in the direction we came from. He says, "Now, imagine a group of people walking exactly as we are right now, down a perfectly sloped hill. The hill itself is just steep enough to cause the group to need to pay careful attention to how they're walking but not too steep as to prevent the very activity of thought. Now, imagine that one of these individuals who is walking down the hill—in between the quick safe steps he or she takes so as not to tumble downhill—mentally trips instead. In other words, their mind lunges where their body is tense and they think a thought completely unrelated to their customary thoughts. The result being a mental free-fall."

The image that comes to my mind is one of a boy tripping on his own momentum, snowballing into a heap of bloody bones and swollen flesh.

"Stubb, listen, your thoughts, your mind, your ideas, they're all useless if you only treat them like a film reel—watching, oohing, ahhing—like a spectator who observes but never creates. Thoughts need movement son. They need tension. They need momentum. They need an unexpected push—a slope which is steep."

"And that's, that's why you like this hill?"

"More or less . . ."

Yesterday, when Papou and I finally found Yiayia inside St. Sophia's, she knew all about our blundered escapade. I guess it was foolish to think we could hide anything from Norfolk's network of white beehives. Yiayia wrapped Papou's sprained wrist with an ace-bandage while shaking her head and chastising. Honestly, I didn't understand half of what she said. Whenever my grandmother gets emotional, she lapses in and out of Greek. During the car ride back, we tried to think of ways to explain the injury to my father, prepping for the moment where he'd adjust his glasses at the kitchen table and ask "What's that?"

Yiayia and Papou moved in with us in 1995, around the same year my father and I took our first neighborhood walk. Dad was worried that Papou's Parkinson's was becoming too much for his mother to handle alone, so he pressured his parents to move in with us, causing Yiayia and Papou to take over our downstairs master-bedroom, relocating my parents to my upstairs bedroom, and emigrating me to the attic. That way, everyone had a floor to themselves. But ever since my grandparents moved in, there's been a running tension between Dad and Papou. Dad, like Yiayia, would prefer Papou to be safer in his old age, more cautious, more shrewd. In other words, he wants the old trickster to retire his coxcomb.

As Yiayia, Papou, and I were pulling into our U-shaped driveway, we put the finishing touches on our cover-story. What happened was that a giant man with giant bushy eyebrows carrying a giant tray of butter cookies accidentally ran into Papou, knocking the old man's wheelchair over, causing him to cushion his fall with his wrist and sprain it. On a positive note, each of us was awarded a delicious *koulourakia* in compensation. According to the cover-story . . .

When we reach the bottom of the hill, Dad makes a confession. He says, "Monday, August 12th, 1974, I was biking home from an internship, that's when it happened, that's when I realized I loved your mother. Sweating profusely, mind unguarded, I came perhaps to my best discovery. Do you understand?"

"You want me to tumble downhill?"

"Mentally . . ."

We continue heading in the direction we came from, passing familiar landmarks along the way: Peasley Elementary School, Mr. Henderson's blind dog, the stop sign with a Metallica sticker on the back, my godmother's eight foot tall "it looks like I'm hiding a dinosaur in my backyard" fence.

For all the walks we've been on, Dad, he still tries to pick away at my layers, to reveal what he believes to be there, hidden inside. To him, a seed is lodged within, a pocket of potential underneath the rind and skin—as opposed to the more likely alternative of an inchworm.

I received a letter from Mark today. The paper had an aged quality to it, as if my best friend had sat down and dabbed its surface with a coffee-stained napkin. Mark informed me that he met with Ethelmar the Wise—Hagerstown's renowned hydromancer. Unfortunately, the visit didn't go as well as expected. To begin with, Ethelmar insisted that the absence of the physical presence of the man to whom the question pertained would decrease the accuracy of the reading significantly. Secondly, he was out of walnut oil. And Ethelmar was convinced that my particular predicament could only be unraveled with walnut oil. That said, he proceeded to pour a few drops of canola oil into a basin of water and then read the shapes which formed below. But the only image he could make out was the state of Pennsylvania. Mark finished his letter by saying that he had a plan, a big plan, a brilliant plan. His P.S. read: "Feathers make poor pens."

A breeze picks up from behind, animating the flora of our neighborhood. Gumballs roll about the concrete like suburban tumbleweed. I can feel my legs getting heavier, my mind becoming lightheaded. According to Dad's most recent lecture, the technical term for this is "the fertile moment where the mind escapes due to decreased surveillance."

What my father wants to create with these walks is an atmosphere of free-association, a climate of eager porousness. But he was right the first time: I'm a spectator—the kind he was condemning just minutes earlier, the kind who ooh's and aah's, the kind who sits ever so quietly in the back row. Even at the University of Maryland, if I had a choice between a lecture and a discussion class, there would be no second thoughts. Shadowed and safe, I would sit in the lecture hall without anxiety, eager to learn non-participatory thoughts.

Dad asks how the new medication is working.

"It's fine," I say. "Just makes me a little groggy, that's all. Compared to the side-effects of most drugs, it's a breeze."

The first medication to effectively eliminate my seizures had the unfortunate side-effect of dunking my head into a vat of molasses. Keppra, in comparison, is pretty good. *Two fat orange pills a day keeps the demon away*—that's how Keppra should advertise. In fact, last week was the first real fit I've had since taking the drug. Dr. Markham and I decided to give Keppra a shot when my seizures returned during my sophomore year at UMD. I was down to about one fit a year—if that. According to Dr. Markham, I was "unlearning" how to have them. But then, suddenly, Papou couldn't walk anymore. And I, I couldn't stand still anymore.

Dad asks if I'm having any headaches.

"Not really."

"Nausea?"

"No."

"Mood swings?"

"Don't think so."

Dad, he just wants to help. I know that. He wants to sow a thirst in his son—a Faustian thirst. He wants to sow a gumption in his son—a Promethean gumption. He wants to sow an impetus in his son, an impetus which—to quote his favorite poet—sees life "as a song one sings before one's throat is cut" . . . And while one could argue that these are the same seeds he wants to uproot from his father, what he's really after is moderation. Like a good

Aristotelian. But what he doesn't understand is that when Papou's gone, it'll just be me. I'm not like them. I'm not even like Mark. I don't "contain multitudes." I'm a different persona for different people because I let each of them strap on whatever mask they please. But they inevitably pocket the personas when they leave. And then, all that's left is the indentation—me.

What Dad doesn't understand is that I've rummaged through the masks. I've tried them all on. I know how they fit. Once Papou's gone, his mask will go with him. But his was the one I most wanted to keep, for it's the one that fit the least.

CHAPTER 8

When Mark returned from Hagerstown, he divulged his plan. He said it was imperative we embark on a journey to Punic. I asked what "Punic" was. He said a small town in Pennsylvania. I asked why it was imperative we visit a small town in Pennsylvania, suggesting that it sounded like the opposite of imperative. He said Punic hosts the largest SCA event of the year, an event where an oracle—Delphic Inc.—known throughout the Kingdom of Atlantia for its prescient profundity, sets up shop once a year. I asked why the kingdom had such a lame name. He complained that I was like a man who had been shot by an arrow but who refused to accept medical assistance until I knew who shot me, why they shot me, when they shot me, what they had for dinner the night before they shot me, and what color their piss was the morning they shot me. I said he stole that analogy from someone, but I didn't know who. He said, "Dude, stop dicking around with destiny." He had a point. So we pulled out a calendar and began planning our itinerary.

It's not that Mark has a "grass is always greener" complex. It's that, at birth, the Fates severed him from his biological parents and spliced his tattered threads with the coiled wires of wanderlust.

We wanted to bring Papou along. Mark and I weren't sure why, but we knew the Aesop rabies and my grandfather were intertwined. Besides, it would give the old trickster a chance to escape from the house. "Old people are like dogs," I've heard Papou say more than once, "they need walks, *Kalo Pathee*, they need a chance to puff up their chest and bark at other old people."

Mark sold Papou on the idea by catering to his funny bone, promising my grandfather that if he could give us four days of his time, we could film a hokey reenactment of the Trojan War in

Pennsylvania which Papou could then sell at his church's Greek festival—this being both a plausible and time-sensitive issue: St. Helen's throws their festival only two weeks after St. Sophia's. The offer itself was especially tempting to the old trickster because of two major hindrances regarding his favorite Greek festival pastime: a sprained wrist and a broken bouzouki.

The next problem was permission slips. Mark and I needed to find people to cover for us at work. Papou needed to get not only his wife's blessing but his son's as well. Luckily, that's where Mom stepped in. Mom's susceptible to Mark, so it didn't take much convincing on Mark's side to enlist her aid. She likes to call him her "other son." As always, Mom shot from the hip. She accused Dad of being a prison warden. She accused Yiayia of being a taxidermist. She accused the house of being Alcatraz. In no time, Papou was given his release.

We left a week later, pulling into our Pennsylvania motel, exhausted from six hours of inactivity. Typically, Mark wouldn't be caught dead at a motel for an SCA event. He'd pack his camping gear and join the other groundlings instead. But knowing we were bringing Papou along, we booked a handicapped room at the nearest motel. There, we're able to assist Papou as he dismounts from his wheelchair to the toilet. There, we can guide his immersion into the bathtub as he attempts to erase our presence from his mind and bathe with the forgotten dignity of a man who doesn't require drowning monitors.

Today is day two of four. We have approximately one day and one morning left to construct a life-size Trojan Horse, recruit a volunteer cast of actors, film a camcorder blockbuster, and consult an oracle of the Delphic variety.

Some might find this schedule constricting or stressful. But Papou, Mark, and I, we've acquiesced to the "shirker's syllogism":

a) Work will get done eventually
b) What we have to do is work
c) What we have to do will get done eventually

Holding the metal poles of my grandfather's augmented wheelchair, I walk forward, pulling Papou like a handcart. The old man rides shirtless, his white curly hair covering his chest in permanent surfs. A folded cloak lies on Papou's lap while an eyepatch covers his right eye. He yells out: "*Okniros!*" and "*Skylos!*"—"lazy!" and "dog!" His character is a pirate named "Constantine the One-Eyed," a fictional 16th century Mediterranean sea-dog.

Personas are a must at Punic. Mothers comfort their children by saying: "Just *don't* be yourself." Individuals are given a chance to cultivate their second life, to groom what they might have been once upon a time in a land far far away. At the Closet of Comics, we do this all the time. We create character cards and personalities for role-playing games. Some—like my boss—prefer to add defects to their characters in order to gain more overall points which they can then distribute to more positive attributes, like "strength," "charisma," "willpower," or "intelligence." Myself, I prefer grounded characters with moderate statistics.

The only other time Papou and I visited an SCA event was the year Mark and I graduated. After inspecting the uninspiring but historically accurate tunics which Mark picked out for us, Papou and I decided to rent costumes from the mall. I chose a one-size-fits-all outfit of King Arthur. Papou went as Merlin, dressing up in a shiny blue robe with white stars. When Yiayia dropped us off at the SCA campground, we exited the car, holding tinfoil accoutrements: a wand for Papou, Excalibur for myself. Mark almost had a heart attack when he saw us. To this day, I've never seen him so mortified. He ushered us to the trunk of his car where he forced us to change our clothes into earth-colored cowls.

This time, we've sought Mark's approval. We make our way through Punic in authentic "period" costumes. No wands. No tinfoil. No stars. My costume is a burgundy tunic with wooden buttons. My character: an 11th century Slavic peon named "Zug-Zug." For accuracy's sake, I've smeared mud over my body.

Papou and I are on a quest of sorts. We're looking for a mead-hall called "Herod's." According to the Barn—Punic's information desk—we need to cut through the Academy to reach the Vittler's District, where we should be able to find the Blackfriar's Amphitheater. There, adjacent to the amphitheater, is Herod's, where Mark said he'd rendezvous with us at seven.

Thanks to an anachronistic epidemic, the town of Punic's population has ballooned from 2,000 to 12,000, the vast majority of which is quarantined in one place: the campgrounds of Cradle Lake. The whole setting is like an alternate dimension, a place where time-travelers of all eras—common and uncommon—congregate in a Dungeons and Dragons sort of way and drop their historical prejudices and mingle in a Woodstock sort of way: Mongolian tartars sharing tents with Gallic swordsmen, Swedish berserkers sharing skillets with Parthian bowmen, Irish druids sharing alcohol with Nubian spearmen.

Mark could be anywhere. Maybe he's fighting a capture-the-flag battle in the Melee District. Or perhaps he's off in the Merchants' Quarters, peddling his homemade wares, trying to pocket some extra cash. Or maybe he's lying down in the Chirurgeon's tent, cringing in pleasure, enduring a deep-tissue massage.

This morning, at a dirt field known as "The Scrapyard," we began construction of our future film's most important prop: the Trojan Horse. Using Mark's limited connections, we were able to acquire a bric-a-brac of basic building blocks: a set of tan bedsheets, a wheelbarrow of recycled cardboard boxes, a bundle of 2×4s, and a can of sea-green paint. As of two hours ago, the horse's equine exoskeleton stood at a wobbly four-and-a-half feet tall and resembled a gift to the god of curbside pickups.

Papou and I arrive at the Academy, Punic's education district. Adults scurry about, holding their children's hands, late for class. The Academy is comprised of a vast plot of teepees—eight rows of cone-shaped crops. In tent 43, Lady Rachel runs a workshop on "Norwegian Nursery Rhymes." In tent 51, Olwen the Odd teaches people "How to Start a Fire like a Moderately Intelligent Saxon." In tent 62, Master Edwyn lectures on "Your Persona's Religion."

I scan my crumpled map, suddenly struck by the absurd hope that someone's running a seminar on "Drafting Peppy Aesop Fables."

These days, fervently doodling Aesop animals in my little notepad is second-nature—like eating lunch, brushing my teeth, or taking a shit. Unfortunately, when it comes to writing and not drawing, the only peppy fable I've been able to come up with is ridiculous, not joyous. It involves a lemming named Lemmy Lemmanuel Lemini L. Lemmy is skeptical of his family's tradition of plunging off cliffs, despite his parents' insistence that it's a time-honored tradition. When Lemmy questions why no lemming has ever returned after plunging off their family's cliff, his parents retort: "Why would they?! Below us is a better place!" When Lemmy asks how they know that below them is a better place, his parents respond: "Literally, the valley is called 'A Better Place'!" But despite all this, Lemmy remains skeptical, torn. He dreams of being an explorer someday, like his great great great great grandfather before him, Lemmy Lemmanuel Lemini XXVI, who supposedly never left home without a bundle of flags in case he stumbled upon, perchance, an uncharted crag. One day, without his parents' permission, Lemmy sets off to find what "A Better Place" really is. Enlisting the help of his friend, Mohandas Mole, he burrows down to the bottom of the cliff and finds out, to his dismay, that "A Better Place" is really a final resting place. The moral—*Look before you leap*. Or—*Names can be deceiving*. Or—*Be wary of the bandwagon fallacy*. Or—*1 out of every 50 lemmings isn't retarded*. Or—*Whatever the fuck will get me to stop scribbling little talking animals like a goddamn psychopath . . .*

Papou and I make our way through the Academy, trying to keep our rubber-necking and ogling to a minimum. We're already late. Once we reach the Vittler's District, it doesn't take us long to find Herod's. Recalling Mark's advice, we simply follow the music of Jethro Tull. Greeted by a tiny anticlimactic sign, we come face to face with the tent. Two rows of porta potties line Herod's like sordid sentinels. With the sun slipping into the periphery of the horizon, we enter the tent.

A crowd of 50 or so fellow patrons huddle around picnic tables, each paying homage to that old Epicurean creed: eating, drinking, and merry-making. The scene resembles the *Star Wars* intergalactic cantina of Mos Eisley. Except, instead of playing host to an infamous hive of scum and villainy, Herod's hosts a rather benign comic book convention, a place where Gauls eat tofu, Huns sip micro-brews, and Dragoons wear glasses.

Papou and I make our way to the back and find Mark sitting red with exhaustion. He's holding a goblet of honey mead, dressed in a steel breastplate, steel leggings, and a white tunic. Resting on the seat beside him is a crimson horsehair-crested helmet, a long oval wooden shield, and a blunt wooden short sword. Mark greets us and starts describing the creative non-fiction battle he's just partaken in, showing off a few of his bruises as he narrates the defense of the city of Antioch. I assume when he says the word "Antioch," what he's referring to is one of the straw-thatched rectangular forts near the western parking lot.

After dismantling Papou's handcart, I order a mead for Papou and a water for myself.

Mark asks if we're ready . . .

Last night, we decided to plan our entertainment a day in advance. We agreed to perform a symposium at Herod's. I guess it sounded like something our personas would do. And today's the day. The agreed upon topic was "love." Each of us was to prepare a speech in praise of love.

Mark suggests I go first.

"Wait, why do I go first?"

"Youngest to oldest."

"What about alphabetical? Odds and evens? Rock, paper, scissors?"

"I don't follow . . ."

"Look, all I'm saying is that there *are* other ways of determining order . . ."

Despite these protests, Papou and Mark hold firm.

"Fine," I say, "is, uh, is there something I should do before I start?"

Mark suggests a title.

Papou lifts his goblet in the air, suggesting a toast.

I lift my water in response and begin . . .

"According to some authoritative source that I can't name at the moment, love was invented by the troubadours—"

Mark asks if that was my title.

"Is heckling allowed?"

We turn to Papou.

He says, "Only if it's funny . . ."

"So, Mark can't heckle anymore?"

"Shut up, Killjoy."

"Anyways, what I want to argue is that love is a bit of revenge, a devious invention inspired by the muse of resentment. But let's backtrack first. You might be asking yourself: 'Who were the troubadours?' Well, they were lower-class musicians and poets of the Middle Ages. Okay, they weren't *all* from the lower classes, but it helps my argument to pretend they were. Anyways, being in the lower classes was shitty and not much fun, as you might have guessed. So what the troubadours did in order to cope with their allotted shittiness was to take revenge on the aristocrats of the day, who they saw as the authors of their shittiness. So the troubadours started singing about an amazing unparalleled force which propels one to do anything for another person—especially destructive and crazy things like walking across a bridge of swords or leaping into a pit of snakes or killing one's king . . . Of course, the object of this force had to be someone who was unattainable, someone taboo, someone either guarded by a dragon or betrothed to another person—which, I guess, is like being guarded by a dragon . . . Anyways, the aristocrats ate it up. They loved it. They loved 'love.' They couldn't have enough of it. They began trying to emulate the troubadours' songs by doing reckless and crazy things, like waging wars on distant kingdoms and committing adultery with the spouses of their fellow aristocrats. And, as you can imagine, all of this was really funny to the troubadours, who, through the simple invention of a word, had been able to manipulate those above them like puppets. But it gets worse . . .

The tradition of the troubadours didn't die with them. It actually lives on in the 21st century with Hollywood screenwriters. In particular, with the writers of romantic comedies. And God knows I have no idea why these people do what they do, but they insist of taking revenge on the general public. Maybe they can't get laid, and so they don't want anyone else to get laid? I have no idea. But whatever the reason, they're taking revenge on the modern age, creating characters called soul-mates who are so preposterously perfect that those who watch romantic comedies are warped into thinking their beloved will actually live up to these standards, condemning each and every one of us to a lifetime of failed romantic expectations . . ."

Mark asks if I'm finished.

"Yeah, I think so . . ."

We ask Papou if we're supposed to clap or something like that.

He says, "Only if they're good . . ."

Papou claps.

Mark doesn't.

I call Mark a dick.

He laughs and then clears his throat and begins . . .

"Most stories say that Love was a god. They got that part right. The rest—not so much . . . The truth is that Love, as an infant, was sent floating down the river of the underworld in a basket of straw—"

"Hack . . ."

"Killjoy, there's a difference between 'motif' and 'hack'."

Papou, frustrated, waves his hands in the air.

I guess all true storytellers are fourth-wall conservationists.

"So," Mark continues, "like I was saying, Love was found floating on the river of the underworld. Now, the ferryman of the underworld was the one who discovered Love. This kind of thing was actually a daily occurrence for him. Every mother this side of myth ditched their unwanted children down the river of the underworld. They all thought they were being original, but they weren't: the river of the underworld was as original as today's 'knock-knock, baby's there'. But luckily for Love, the ferryman had a soft spot in his heart for orphans. Some said he was one himself, but all that's certain is that he collected little foundlings and raised them on a great big orphanage barge. Now, these children grew up imitating their adopted father, rowing the dead across the river of the underworld, just like him. And at first, Love, he was just another child on the barge. But the ferryman had suspicions he was really a god, for what came with the infant in his basket was a pair of wings, a quiver of arrows, and a golden bow. So, when Love asked the ferryman if he would help him find his mother, the ferryman agreed, knowing that he couldn't keep a god cooped up on his barge forever. Using water hydraulics, the ferryman built an obsidian catapult. The idea was that all Love really needed was a push and then he could fly the rest of his way to the land of the gods. So that's what they did: they flung Love up in the air like a cannonball aimed at the heavens and let him flutter the rest of the way. When Love finally reached his destination, he went to work. He started shooting arrows at any and all females who looked like they could be his mother. And whoever was struck by one of his arrows would fall instantly in love with the first person they laid eyes on, which meant that Love had to do jumping jacks in front of them so that the first person would be him . . . Not that this always worked . . . Sometimes, the women would see an owl flying overhead or their own reflection in a nearby mirror, and then they'd fall in love with those things instead. But there was a bigger problem still, a deeper problem: Love had limited arrows. There was no way he could shoot every maternal-looking goddess out there. Not to mention every nymph, sprite, dryad, and all the other potential demigods that might have been his mother. Love's mission was doomed to fail from the start. So he sat down at the edge of the land of the gods, his legs dangling in the vast emptiness of heaven and lamented the fact that he would never really know if he had hit the woman who had thrown him away. He then put his last arrow in a basket of straw, tied a parachute to it, and let it drop. And the arrow floated down, landed upside down in the oceans below, and punctured the waves. Humans drank the water and arbitrarily fell in love . . ."

"Well, *that* was depressing . . ." I say.

"I thought yours was more depressing . . ."

"We should give an award for the most depressing."

"Yeah . . ."

We fall silent and nurse our drinks.

Herod's patrons continue to trickle in, swelling the mead-hall's population to high-occupancy. Candles are lit by waiters. Jethro Tull's *Aqualung* is replaced with *Thick as a Brick*. The sun is supplanted by the moon in the paragon of pale substitutes.

A group of individuals scoot closer. Their costumes are more fantasy-based than historical. Two of them wear wicca dresses; the other two sport angel wings. Mark puts his shield and helmet under the table to make space. The SCA purist in him cringes.

Knowing that it's his turn, Papou takes a sip of mead and bats the air with his hands. He whispers, "Love, love's a lack . . ." The old man's head bobs as if he's trying to shake water out of his ears. He says, "Only dunderheads think it comes from the heart. Everyone else knows that love comes from the bellybutton. The bellybutton is the heart of lack. When we love others, we love the *other* in them. Maybe it's their face, maybe it's their humor, maybe it's their madness—it doesn't matter what. The fact of the matter is: we don't have it, and we want it, so we love it. I know it sounds bad at first, real twisted like. But it's what makes growing possible, boys—love's the bridge from this to that. But there's no such thing as self-love, boys. That kind of talk is bologna, claptrap. Self-love doesn't make any sense. You can't *not* have yourself. That's the one thing you're stuck with. But there *is* no-love. That makes sense. Trust me, I've seen it. We used to call him 'The Man Who Murdered Love'. His real name was Sava. He was a friend of mine from the restaurant. A real Romeo-pendulum, he was always falling in and out of love. Sava would scrub his skin with basil and dress up all nice. Then, he'd go out on the town, rubbing up against everything like a cat. But there was one relationship which did Sava in. I never found out the details, but I guess it doesn't matter. There was no arrow-hole in his chest or anything like that. No, but his bellybutton was stuffed—the wound had healed. Sava stopped going out. He stopped scrubbing basil on his skin. He stopped dressing up all nice. He just closed his eyes, plugged his ears, stuffed his nose, and gagged his mouth. The only books Sava read anymore were the ones about pathetic characters. The only movies he saw anymore were the ones about losers, lowlifes. That way, there was nothing for Sava to lack. But love, *real* love, that's different, boys. That's hard. It's not easy being with someone who makes you feel like Swiss cheese all the time. But that's what love is, right? That's what we're after—we're looking for someone to make us feel incomplete . . ."

CHAPTER 9

"If you could fill out the form as accurately as possible," says a bearded middle-aged man dressed in a white toga, "the oracle will be with you shortly."

I take hold of the outstretched questionnaire. I ask if under "name" I should use my persona's name or my real name. Or, for that matter, my birth name . . .

Eyes two seas of bloodshot tranquility, the man responds, "Whatever you believe, sir, will best serve in aiding the oracle's powers of perception." He then informs me that our conversation is over by making Spock's *live long and prosper* symbol with his left hand, moving on to assist the pilgrims standing in line behind me.

"Thanks," I say.

This—waiting in line outside Delphic Inc.'s freelancing tent in southwest Pennsylvania—is the best option I have, according to Mark, of aligning my understanding with the all-encompassing whirlpool of Providence. Apparently, all I have to do is wait for my chance to hand the oracle my paperwork and, presto, my problems will be solved, like a microwaveable solution. No more fear. No more depression. No more doodles. Just clear sailing from here on out. One steady gale of serotonin.

The pilgrim in front of me is wearing a purple frock and an ornamental hat with a veil attached to the back which drapes down to her shoulder-blades. Her headgear is difficult to describe. It's like a pair of "bridal horns." She finishes her lunch on the go, the grease dripping from her fried drumstick to the yellow tarp below us, a tarp which is fastened to the grass with sod-staples and forms a winding pathway a quarter of a mile long, auspiciously ending—as yellow trails are wont to do—with a prophetic residence, a green tent. Six other lost souls precede this woman, each of them waiting their turn to hand their questionnaires over to the priest, who will then enter the oracle's emerald tent and hand them over to the priestess, who will then, most likely, get busy inhaling artificial profundity while thinking up ambiguous answers to her clients' predicaments.

I check the "yes" box on my patient information sheet under question 3—*Is this your first visit to Delphic Inc.?*

Question 4 reads: *Which other forms of divination have you sought in the past two years?*

I scan the three columns of unchecked boxes. Fortunately, they're labeled. The answers range from astrology to dendromancy—a form of divination based on the rustling of oak leaves—to chiromancy—a form of divination based on studying an individual's palms.

After studying my options, I check "hydromancy" and "tasseomancy," the latter being a form of divination derived from the interpretation of coffee grinds. It also happens to be an art which Yiayia practices whenever a family get-together involves Turkish coffee.

A typical reading of my grandmother's might go something like this. First, she'll wait for her volunteer to finish their coffee, asking them to remember to keep a little liquid inside the cup in order to facilitate the movement of the omniscient dregs inside. Second, she'll place an upside-down saucer atop the volunteer's cup and then, after saying "*Stin iya su!*" or "Cheers!" she'll flip over the mug, allowing the grinds time to drip down the walls of the cup like drops of a viscous future oozing into a porcelain present. Last, she'll turn the cup aright, point the handle of the mug in the direction of the seated volunteer, and then proceed to tell their future. Maybe she'll see animals inside the cup's black canvas which will symbolize an event in that person's near future. Or maybe she'll uncover a few letters spelling out a name, a watchword. Whatever the case, she'll close her eyes, take a deep breath, and foretell either impending doom or prolonged prosperity. And being a benevolent old lady at heart, you can bet on prolonged prosperity. My grandmother, she's probably the most untrustworthy midwife to the gods imaginable.

I pull my notepad out of my pocket and scribble a reminder to myself to call this old benevolent tasseomancer when we get back to the motel. Yiayia prefers that we call her once a day to give her updates on Papou.

Question 5 reads: *Take 100-200 words to describe your condition . . .*

My condition . . . This is where multiple choice comes in handy. Or process of elimination. Or those previous columns of unchecked boxes . . .

- ☐ *My condition is that I fear mortality . . .*
- ☐ *My condition is that I'd like not to murder my father and marry my mother . . .*
- ☐ *My condition is that I'm not in Kansas anymore . . .*
- ☐ *My condition is that my current condition is neither necessary nor sufficient . . .*
- ☐ *My condition is that I want to exchange conditions . . .*
- ☐ *I want to speak to the Oracle's manager . . .*

That's all most people want. An educated guess. The opportunity to see the answer in front of them like a police lineup and to declare behind the safety of bulletproof glass: "That one! It was that one: they did it! They're the ones who are responsible for my *condition*!"

But since there's no choices to help me out, I write a short essay in the blank below, describing how I woke up one morning with the intractable urge to doodle Aesop animals. I explain how this urge hasn't gone away, how I sketch the animals on a daily basis, how my best friend is convinced that it means something big, how I'm skeptical that it means anything at all, how I sometimes draw my grandfather along with the animals, how I'm tired of being skeptical all the time, how my father asked me to write a fable four years ago, how I wrote three inadequate drafts, how I'm trying to write a new peppy fable which will set everything right, how I'm not crazy, how my grandfather is the only person I know who's ever been able to take a lifetime illness and hoodwink the fucker into submission, how I lack the courage to affirm . . .

I conclude the questionnaire with a generic cry for help: "*Oracle, what does it all mean?*" I then check the final box which asks for an additional ten dollars in order to provide the answer in rhyming couplets.

An M-shaped metal archway over seven feet tall stands before the priestess' tent. Each pilgrim, when it's their turn to be seen by the oracle, enters through the right archway. When they've received their answer on a roll of papyrus, they exit through the left. What I've gathered from a brief conversation with the portly samurai behind me is that this edifice is here to represent the navel of the world, the point where we mortals were sundered from the umbilical cord of the gods. When I asked the same samurai what Delphic Inc. does during the remaining 50 weeks of the year, he answered: "infomercials."

There's actually a connection between Delphi and Aesop. It's where the poor bastard meets his end. Aesop is framed in Delphi, accused of theft, and tossed off a cliff. So, I guess it's only fitting if Delphic Inc. is the one who chucks my Aesop rabies off a cliff . . .

After a late breakfast, I left Papou and Mark somewhere around the nipple of the world. I conceded to them the honor of recruiting volunteer thespians for our upcoming film about the fall of Troy, a film whose shooting schedule might be the most limited in film history: our hours of operation running from 9:00 am to 10:00 am tomorrow morning—rain or shine, lines memorized or not, volunteers or no. Thanks to a white lie, I've managed to dodge the acting bullet by convincing Mark of my camcorder skills. Papou, on the other hand, has fully embraced his role in the movie, purchasing a bag of blood capsules in anticipation of playing King Priam: the king who loses. Mark, due to expected cast limitations, will play over half of the Greek army, including Odysseus, Diomedes, and Pyrrhus: the soldiers who murder Papou.

The air mingles as we near the oracle's green tent. A gamut of scents can be detected, aromas ranging from pot to incense to turkey grease to body odor to the garlic breath of the priest in charge of the questionnaires. All of this serves to confirm my earlier suspicion that it would've been a bad idea to smear animal feces over my peasant's tunic in an attempt to be more "period."

The woman in front of me turns around. Holding up her drumstick, she asks if I know of anywhere to throw away her bone. Her hair is dark brown, but her roots betray a sandy color underneath. Her eyelashes and eyebrows are defined in a light coating of mascara. She has a small beauty mark on her nose: a metal ring. Around her neck is a griffin pendant.

When we were in high school, Mark introduced me to a system of measuring beauty which uses a unit called "Hellenes." The system is based off of Helen of Troy—the face that launched a thousand ships. Simply put, one Hellene is a beauty capable of launching one ship. Now, that might sound harsh at first, but the vast majority of us don't even register on the Hellene scale. At best, we're capable of launching a message in a bottle.

"I, I guess I can hold on to the drumstick for you?" I say.

She looks roughly my age. Early 20's. About 40 Hellenes.

"That's just weird," she says.

"I, I meant to say that my character would be someone who *would* take it, theoretically. 'Cause, you know, your character looks like nobility while mine—"

"Why? Who are you?"

"A Slavic peon from the 11th century known as 'Zug-Zug'. By his friends . . ."

"Oh."

"My parents were captured and sold into slavery by a Viking raid when I was three."

"I'm sorry. I didn't know . . ."

"It's okay. It was a long time ago."

"Now, when you say 'Vikings', are you referring to the forces of Harold Bluetooth or do you mean more like Sweyn Forkbeard or

King Cnut?"

"I, I kind of just lump them all together under the term 'Northmen'."

"Oh . . ."

"You're, you're not a Northwoman, are you?

"No, I'm . . . my character's from France. Michelle of Ghent. I'm a lady in waiting for Queen Isabeau."

"Isabel? Like the queen of Spain?"

"No, 'Isabeau'. She's the queen of France during the time of Joan of Arc."

"Right. I knew that . . . Doesn't she marry a king of England or something like that? Richard III, II, IV?"

"You're thinking of Henry V. He marries Isabeau's daughter. Henry marries Catherine of France just before dying of dysentery."

"Dysentery—I always forget what dysentery is . . ."

"Inflammation of the colon. Lethal diarrhea."

The more Michelle and I talk, the more two things become painfully obvious: Michelle's done her homework, and I haven't. Which is funny because I always thought my only chance of making it with a beautiful woman would be to make it with a dorky one. But "dork" is a misunderstood term. Most people treat it like a continuum, as if all dorks resided in the same castle. But it's much more of a spectrum. Take a few steps in any direction and you're suddenly on completely different wavelengths. Take a few more steps and you can't even see each other anymore. Let alone communicate . . .

My guess is that if I was ever going to woo a dorky beautiful woman, it would have to be within the narrow wavelength of the Closet of Comics, a wavelength where I could hold her spellbound as I led her through the winding labyrinth of DC's *Crisis on Infinite Earths*, delineating the ins and outs of the most convoluted mini-series of all time.

When the conversation lulls, Michelle turns around, avoiding the awkwardness of facing another person without talking.

I look up. Cirrus clouds leave streaks of white in an otherwise blue sky. It looks like the aftermath of a stratospheric race.

After all that talk about love yesterday, here I am, at the bellybutton of the world, at the wellspring of lack, and what am I doing but closing my eyes, plugging my ears, stuffing my nose, gagging my mouth . . .

Thank God Papou's not here.

Michelle walks through the oracle's arches and hands her questionnaire over to the priest.

Sewn into the top of the oracle's emerald tent is an official statement of prophetic credentials in golden cursive: "I count the grains of sand on the beach and measure the sea; I understand the dumb and hear the voiceless."

Michelle, after a few minutes, is given her papyrus scroll and sent on her way. She curtsies to me on her way out, which is more than old Zug-Zug would historically deserve.

The priest motions for me to walk through the right archway. I hand him my questionnaire and wait in front of the oracle's tent for an answer, attempting to peek inside, unsuccessfully. I imagine the priestess and her aids are smoking a hookah and drafting my fate.

Pacing like a man in a waiting room, I glance anywhere, everywhere. I stare at the line of pilgrims behind me—a motley group of modern-day Ishmaels and Esaus, Dorothys and Scarecrows, Oedipi and Oresti. This is the lot of every lost soul: sooner or later, you get to the point where you can't help it anymore, so you pay a stranger to tell you how it all went wrong.

The priest emerges from the oracle's tent and hands me a rolled-up papyrus. I hand the priest a twenty dollar bill, thank him, and start walking back in the direction I came from. But a half-mile down the road, I curse aloud, unable to shake the sinking suspicion that prophecy is one of those professions where tipping is expected and that this breach in protocol will adversely affect the answer written on my scroll . . .

CHAPTER 10

When we arrived this morning at "The Scrapyard" to shoot our future blockbuster before heading home, we discovered a slight dint in our plan. Or, to be more literal, a rather noticeable decapitation: the head of our homebuilt Trojan Horse had fallen off, either of its own accord or due to some SCA bacchanalian revelry. In any event, what was verifiable was that a splintered neigh in between the hours of 7:00 pm and 7:00 am had given birth to "Stumpy," the headless horseman's faithful steed.

As our eight volunteers for the film gradually trickled in, Mark diffused the situation by taking advantage of the moment, editing the script, changing the film's opening scene from a shot of the wooden horse being inspected by jeering Trojans to a shot of the horse's head lopped off and lying in the dirt. The shot then pans out and reveals the horse's trunk, a trunk ominously surrounded by Greek soldiers who have "vomited" themselves out of the wooden monstrosity.

It's five minutes before showtime.

Mark huddles Papou, myself, and our volunteers into a circle and begins an obligatory motivational speech.

"Friends, volunteers, thespians," he says, "I've not come this far—400 miles—to make a home video. I've come to make the greatest B-movie of all time. Now, who's with me?"

Two volunteers beat their weapons against their shields in encouragement.

Mark continues, quoting the epitaph of the Battle of Thermopylae: "*Go tell the Spartans,*" he says, "*stranger passing by, that here obedient to their laws, we lie.* When people in the future make pilgrimages to this site, they're going to see a monument with an inscription of that epitaph, except, instead of 'Spartans', it's going to say 'Fanboys', and instead of 'lie', it's going to say 'shot the most epic movie ever'."

Two more volunteers let out a cheer.

A third says, "Let's do this!"

Another: "Whatever you say, boss . . ."

Papou responds by drumming his wheelchair like a madman.

I raise my fist with one hand, sipping my coffee with the other.

Papou, for his role as King Priam, has taken off his former character's eyepatch and replaced it with a steel crown, an accessory which—like all the other accessories we've managed to scrounge up for today's performance—Mark has had to finagle from various SCA connections. Six of our volunteers showcase authentic hoplite armor, mail consisting of 40 pounds of shield, breastplate, helmet, and legging weight. Each of these volunteers also wields a wooden spear tipped with a thick wad of duct tape. To differentiate between the Greek and Trojan actors, we've decided that the four volunteers who are playing the Trojans will go shield-less throughout the film and, to top things off, they'll perform a Trojan "death dance," a dance which will consist of two volunteers perpetually standing and fighting while the other two are perpetually dying and crawling off camera, only to reappear for an endless array of fatal cameos.

Our last two volunteers are draped head to toe in black like puppeteers. Being our special effects crew, it will be their job to pace in the background, waving two cardboard posters in the air: colored red and cut to the shape of flames. As the melee progresses and events spiral out of control, they'll speed up their pacing in response, symbolizing the mounting chaos of the battle scene.

Hand held high, I count down from five and then press the record button on the camcorder . . .

After capturing Mark's improvised pan shot, I focus in on the three Greek soldiers standing next to "Stumpy." The actors waffle their heads as if they've just received a flat horseshoe. Thankfully, this awkwardness is soon broken up by our four Trojan actors entering the scene and shouting, "En garde!"

Mayhem ensues.

Last night, after putting Papou to bed, I went outside with Mark and shared Delphic Inc.'s answer to the mystery of my Aesop rabies, unrolling the papyrus scroll and reading aloud:

A garden you must find
to untie you from this bind—
both a place to bury a seed
and a plot to uproot a weed.
We think it first smart
to toss out a small part
before planting the young oat
to nourish the old note.

I then told Mark that he owed me his firstborn child for making me stand in line and pay twenty dollars for such ambiguous bullshit. Mark shook his head and claimed that he would never hand his firstborn over to a dupe who couldn't differentiate gold from shit.

"It's a riddle—use your head," he said.

"So what the fuck does it mean?"

"No clue."

"What?"

"It is *your* riddle, you know. So how should *I* know what it means?"

"I hate you so much right now . . ."

"A garden . . . Killjoy, think about it, what gardens do you know?"

The on-screen action continues. Middle-aged men move around like turtles, beating one another with wooden clubs as our special effects crew scurry behind the scenes, holding up their red posters, resembling demonic cheerleaders. Meanwhile, the Trojan death-dance trickles down to a shuffle due to its exhaustive nature and to the fact that our volunteers aren't exactly in Olympic shape. In the heat of battle, one of the Greeks undoes his helmet and takes a water break. And who knows, maybe in the future when people consult video dictionaries, this very clip will define the word *Camp (n).*

Mark twirls in mini-cyclones, performing a sequence of spin moves, sword thrusts, and shield bashes, outshining the other actors in athleticism and zealotry. When we were younger, I wasn't just emulating Alexander, Caesar, and Hannibal; I was also emulating Mark. But each seizure was a rattling, an emptying—loose change shaken from a piggy bank. By the 9th grade, Mark was as rich as Croesus, while I had filed for bankruptcy.

Rushing ahead, Mark confronts Papou, who's prematurely bitten his blood capsule, causing his chin to dribble red beads of high fructose corn syrup. The old trickster tries hard to cover up his mouth, but he can only hold back so many cackles before giving in to laughter. Mark, on the other hand, being a veteran when it comes to hokey reenactments, maintains his composure. He says, "King Priam, I presume!"

Papou responds: "Pyrrhus, you dog!"

I step forward and zoom in to the scene. This is our film's one moment of dialogue, which makes it the climax of the movie. Mark and I toyed with writing the lines out beforehand, imitating the *Iliad's* meter of dactylic hexameter, but then we quickly abandoned this idea for the much simpler plan of letting Papou and Mark improvise on-screen.

"Your days of ruling are numbered, old man."

"This is all Stella's fault."

"Helen . . ."

"Helen, right, her too . . ."

Mark points his sword at Papou and asks if he has any last words.

Papou taunts, saying that Mark's character wouldn't dare kill an old man in a wheelchair.

"That's where you're wrong," Mark says. "Dead wrong!" He approaches Papou and stabs him to death.

Twitching, moaning, Papou steers his wheelchair in circles like a melodramatically wounded horse. But even when the old man's done with the scene and wants to be still, he twitches, quivers.

The rest of the story's action is falling.

I watch as the four Trojans, one by one, collapse thankfully to the ground, halting their exhausting death-dance. Every actor—Trojan and Greek alike—is either panting or grunting or huffing or heaving. The feature length of our freshly recorded masterpiece: 10 minutes and 42 seconds.

Mark concludes the film by standing on camera and reading the credits aloud. He acknowledges a mostly fabricated list of special thanks, including executive producers, casting coordinators, directors of cinematography, resident consultants of historical accuracy, and so on and so forth. I think he's padding the running time.

This morning, I woke up earlier than usual. Around 5:30. I couldn't get back to bed, so I stumbled over to the motel lobby and waited for the first cup of coffee to be brewed. I brought my notepad along and sketched the fable of "The Fox and the Grapes." But this time, my drawing was controlled, voluntary. It spanned three panels altogether. The first panel depicted a fox discovering a juicy cluster of grapes drooping from a tree. The second: the fox swiping its paws at the grapes, stretching its body to its vertical limit and panting profusely. The third: the fox giving up, leaving the grapes behind, and muttering: "Eh, they're probably sour anyways . . ."

I couldn't shake the sudden thought that *Aesop is the fox . . . Aesop is the fox. . . Life is the grapes and Aesop is the fox . . .* After all, Aesop was an ugly slave who was unjustly tossed off a cliff. Who wouldn't have a sour taste in their mouth after an experience like that? But why tell the fable? What's the point? Why didn't Aesop just let the experience die? Why give it life?

Mark touches me on the shoulder. He says I can hit the stop button at any time. He removes his helmet and wipes his face with a handkerchief.

"You all right?" he asks.

"Yeah. I'm good."

"Pretty fucking amazing, no?"

"What?"

"The movie . . ."

"Oh, yeah, Oscar worthy, no doubt."

I'm the fox . . . I'm that little furry fucker too . . .

Once upon a time, Stubb came across a juicy cluster of grapes which he couldn't reach, so he had a fit, shook his spray-can, aimed it at the cluster, and doused it. He spoiled them. I spoiled them. It was me. It was Stubb in the attic with the spray-can of resentment.

PART II

THE TORTOISE AND THE EAGLE

CHAPTER 1

On the Sunday mornings of my childhood, my parents would play host to pirates. Just after eight, the first volley of cannon shots would pelt the front door, signaling the arrival of the captain and his first mate. Boarding our house, the two would hail in their vernacular—"*Kaleemera! Kafe!*"

By nine, a handful of shipmates would toss their gangplanks onto our deck and rambunctiously join the fray, converting the kitchen into a galley, the living room into a mess-hall.

By ten, the scallywags had all but hoisted a Jolly Roger up our chimney.

But these were no arbitrary pirates; no, they were blood relatives—aunts and siblings and cousins and parents—who had all come to revel in that buried treasure of heredity. Lying in my bed, I would count how many times my name would be mentioned in between their hooting and guffawing as they pronounced that foreign word "*Stubb*" with facetious wonder, rhyming and punning as they pleased, their voices shaking the crow's nest of my upstairs bedroom.

Succumbing to the pangs of curiosity, I would eventually grip the upstairs banister and begin my long descent, tiptoeing down, watching the shadows dance at the bottom of the stairwell as I resigned myself to an inevitable capture, the captain's large paws grabbing and saddling me on top of his shoulders as he advertised to his mates: "*To kalo pathee! Kalo pathee mou!*" And after having showed off this newest of pilfered booties, the old skipper would then saunter off, attending to pressing buccaneer business, abandoning me to the visibility of the deck—an exposed but familiar stowaway.

There, surrounded by a language I didn't understand, card games I had never played, food I could hardly pronounce, I would stand firm against the wall and think to myself: these people come from another port, a port in which blue-eyed amulets can ward off envy, hard-boiled eggs can harness good luck, and coffee cups can augur the future. I would stand and watch as their mouths gaped open and closed, their nostrils flared in and out, fearing they would asphyxiate the world.

It was only after old Aunt Vula would take me in, pinching my arms, my sides, my ears, and my neck like some maternal lobster, that I would ask the old lady to translate for me, asking her what was so funny that it had caused Uncle Demo to choke on his *loukoumades* or what was so taboo that Aunt Helen found it necessary to shush everyone in the room with an onion-gleaming kitchen knife.

Always a little before noon, the captain and his mob would don their jackets and congregate at the front door, ushering my parents and I outside, where we would travel down the street and up the parking lot to St. Helen's hallowed dome. No longer a shellback but now a full-blown member of the captain's crew, I would take a seat with the other Sunday mates and wait for that man, that ordained bard decked out in a golden robe, to step onto the stage and begin "story-time," a ten minute interval in which tales would be woven in English about saints killing dragons, vagabonds wrestling angels, fishermen healing invalids, and, my personal favorite, the one about how a lowly carpenter rested three days inside a cocoon and awoke on the third day as one of the numerators in God's fraction.

But today, the water is calm, dead.

The pirates: beached, sunk.

The captain docked in the hospital for two days with viral pneumonia.

It's Sunday morning and the past is a jar of expired afterglow.

My attic carpet is littered with crumpled paper, aborted fables—drafts about moles rescuing trapped miners, polar bears solving global warming, squirrels discovering "acornucopias," and beavers abating incoming tsunamis with dams the size of Babel.

Stories . . .

The captain, he once told me that Death was afraid of stories. At the time, my image of Death wasn't that of a man in a cloak with a scythe, but a teacher in a business suit who erased individuals from his chalkboard. Papou insisted that Death was petrified of stories. I asked Papou why he was so scared of stories. He asked me why I was scared of snakes. I said, "They're all slimy and slippery." "So, there you go," he said, "it's the same with Death." "So, stories are slimy and slippery?" "Yeah, and they can shed their skin. And Death's terrified of anything which can shed its skin."

But that was just another story. You can't multiply a story by a story and get a truth. This isn't math. There's no fable I can write to ward off pneumonia, Parkinson's, epilepsy, or death. Let alone, "Aesop rabies." This whole peppy fable idea was so fucking stupid to begin with. Such logorrhea.

At best, truth is anecdotal. If you slide a trampoline under its feet, it can soar to the heights of hearsay . . .

One day, Frederick II wanted to learn what language the angels spoke, so he decided to take a handful of infants and have them raised in a sequestered forest by deaf mutes. The children grew up, to Frederick II's chagrin, deaf and mute. The truth—"We will become our environment."

And that's what's going to happen to me. When Papou's gone, that's what's going to happen to me. All disorders will become standardized. There'll be no other languages to speak. Just my bitten tongue. The indented language of me.

CHAPTER 2

Our swing-set looks like the childhood inspiration of the Brothers Grimm—frayed ropes, rusted hooks, swollen wood, and pendulum creaking. It's hard to imagine that Hansel and Gretel survive in every version of the story. There must be one where they're bound with ivy, gagged with apples, and baked alive. Where the witch lives happily ever after.

Papou's wearing his lint-freckled overcoat and the Russian Cossack hat that drives Yiayia insane. His face, since the hospitalization, has melted and hardened anew, molding into a mask of dumbstruck debility. The old man swings in staggered vibrations.

Mark's head is down. The belt to his green trench coat lies coiled in the dirt below. His motion is mechanical—a timid tick-tock. My best friend swings as if condemned to the gallows.

I'm leaning on the edge of my seat, spading the earth with my toes, attempting to make brunch feasible for the late bird.

The sky is an old gray comforter punctured with tiny holes: the aftermath of a desperate moth in search of a brighter world.

The garlic leaves of Mom's herb garden droop with exhaustion, panting like green tongues.

It hasn't even been two months since our excursion to Pennsylvania, but, somehow, the whole mad adventure—constructing a Trojan Horse out of trash, quaffing mead inside Herod's, visiting Delphic Inc., filming *Troy: the True Story*—it all feels like it was undertaken in another life. The rules are different now, since Papou's hospitalization. Dad and Yiayia would never let us take Papou out for something like that again.

I couldn't help but overhear Yiayia interrogating Papou last night in their bedroom, my grandmother asking her husband why he keeps escaping the house, why he keeps rolling down the street like a dog broken free of its leash, why he's so willing to leave her and depart this world forever . . .

Impatient with our silence, Papou hums aloud. He kicks his feet and rocks his swing. He gives in to the Parkinson's wish to remove all resistors from the circuit. He says, "Some people hum when they're happy. Others when they're nervous. Others when they're bored or scared or when they're standing in front of a public urinal and have to go but can't. Have you ever thought, boys, that *when* we hum says a lot about *who* we are? Or, what does it mean if we never hum at all?"

The maple trees surrounding us are adorned in autumn: pumpkin-orange, apple-red, plum-purple, yam-brown. Even St. Helen's dome in the distance appears aptly seasonal—yet another yellow thing preparing for the apocalypse. I've always admired this cyclical phenomenon, the way the world dresses up in its Sunday best before going skydiving.

"Me," Papou says, "I hum when I'm remembering. It's the only time I feel like closing my lips and saying sound . . ."

Our sales for *Troy: the True Story* were less lucrative than expected. Using Yiayia's connections, we were given a booth inside Saint Helen's Community Center, sandwiched in between a water fountain and the handicapped bathroom. When we tried migrating to the more fertile mercantile grounds of the gymnasium, we were promptly shooed away by rival vendors and told we didn't have a permit to set up shop in the jewelry bazaar. Grudgingly, we stayed put, manning our table on and off for three days, selling a total of eleven DVDs for a net loss—counting food, lodging, and gas to Pennsylvania—of 250 dollars. Mark blamed our sales on our awkward kiosk position. I blamed Mark for insulting our patrons, dressing up as a Roman centurion at a *Greek* festival. Papou blamed our audience's poor taste.

"Did I ever tell you two," Papou continues, "about when I first met Yiayia, about how I wooed her?"

"No, I don't think so," I say.

The old trickster palpitates with a new vigor. He says, "Now, I had seen Cia before. It was a face this young greculio couldn't easily forget. We lived in the same neighborhood of Norfolk, and I knew she was Spartan as well. So, when I got on the bus that day and saw her riding alone, I decided it was time to make my move. I walked up to her and . . . Do you know what I did?"

"No," I say.

"It was quite simple—"

"What did you do?" Mark asks.

"I *sat* on her hat."

"Accidentally?"

"No, no, on purpose, *Kalo Pathee*. It was something my friend Sava had taught me. He used to say, 'Why doff what you can trap?' And it worked like a charm. We started chatting. After a few minutes I had convinced Cia to come with me and get some coffee at the restaurant. But as we were walking down the bus' aisle and were about to exit, the driver turned to Cia and said, 'Miss, don't get off the bus with that man.' " Papou laughs. "You see," he says, "I took that bus every day. The driver, he knew I had more than one devil inside of me. And when devils are concerned, anything over one is a dangerous number. The poor old fool did his best to warn Cia, but it was too late . . ."

Papou lets his swing teeter to a stop. He scans his audience for a response, waffling his head, licking his lips.

Mark asks Papou if he's cold, if he needs another jacket or something like that.

I ask the old man if he's thirsty, if he wants something hot to drink like coffee or tea.

"Xezo!" Papou curses.

"What?"

"If you guys get a bloody nose, do I act like this?!"

"Act like what?"

Papou spits and wipes the saliva off his mouth. "Boys," he says, "I'm not dead *yet* . . ."

"Papou—"

"Doesn't Cia do this enough? Christ, I need you two! For balance . . . No, not for balance! To hell with balance! That's the problem with everything these days. No, for recklessness boys, for *un*-balance." Papou lowers his voice as if preparing a confession. He says, "I need you two to act as if I was immortal . . ."

I tell Papou that we're sorry, that we're just worried.

Mark nods his head in agreement, ever-mortified by the emergence of reality—especially the reality of death. When we were younger and Mark's iguana died, he avoided mentioning the event to me for as long as possible. Eventually, I asked him rather bluntly if "Septor the Surreptitious" had kicked the green bucket. Mark took me to the backyard, opened his pocket knife, and forced me to blade my palm in a blood oath, forbidding me from ever mentioning Septor's name again. And to this day, I never have. I've never mentioned "Septor" since—afraid that I, like Rumpelstiltskin, might perish of a name.

Papou closes his eyes and returns to his previous humming.

I wait for Mark to say something.

Mark waits for me.

A slight breeze picks up, blowing clouds our way which resemble charcoal sponges. Not wolves. Not lambs. Not foxes. Not mice. But charcoal sponges. There's no fables etched in the sky. I'm beginning to think that my Aesop rabies is going into remission. I've gained a certain amount of control over the random doodling. If I sketch a fable of my own volition every other day or so, I find that I don't really need to worry about carrying my notepad around. I can control *when* I doodle—if not *that* I doodle. And I guess there's always the possibility of this trend continuing until the Aesop doodling peters out, expiring in an arbitrary horizontal line or a chance smudge. It wouldn't be the first time an aimless eruption ended in entropy . . .

See the Big Bang.

See the second law of thermodynamics.

See seizures.

See roughly two out of every three cases of epilepsy.

Tucking his chin into his chest, Papou pulls up his overcoat. He says, "Besides, I have this . . ." He outlines a light-brown birthmark on his lower back—a long oval and a small circle. I've never noticed before but the shape, it's a perfect exclamation point. Papou pinches the melatonic punctuation and says, "As long as this remains here, nothing can happen to me . . ."

"Why? What does it do?" I ask.

"Why, bah! Who knows, *Kalo Pathee*? But *how*, I do know a little about that. You see, it all began with one of my great uncles, Theo Pavlos—a real curmudgeon. No one in the family thought Pavlos would ever marry. His mother used to throw her hands in the air and cry, 'Who's unhappy enough to marry Pavlos?!' But a plan was eventually devised to match Theo Pavlos with a widowed mute from Crete. You see, our family, they thought there would be less arguments that way. But this woman from Crete, there was something unnatural about her. Her body was mapped in tattoos; her eyes were like burning pomegranates. Day and night, something kindled inside of her, never quite freeing itself. She died shortly after their marriage, in childbirth, but not before giving birth to Michael—'Michael the Madman' as some called him—and also to one of her tattoos, a mark exactly this shape"— Papou grips his lower back—"a mark which lived on in Michael as a birthmark on his left calf, handed down from mother to son..."

Papou takes a break from his story, gauging his audience's reception before preemptively pleading, "Boys, this is *true* . . ." enunciating the word slowly, smoothly, as if it were the iron to flatten all skeptical creases.

I laugh, which is the storytelling equivalent of a green light.

Mark widens the arc to his swing—the equivalent of a canine wagging its tail.

"So Michael," Papou continues with a smile, "Michael the Madman had this same tattoo on his left calf. And while it's true that Michael wasn't a mute like his mother, they were similar in other ways, for the man's mouth was always on the verge of frothing. He would stumble on the simplest words. When he wanted to communicate, he'd jerk around like a man possessed. All the townsfolk would look to his father for translation, but his father would just shrug and say, 'Michael says he's hungry, Michael says thank you, Michael says he hates you.' One day, the little madman jumped on a ship and sailed God knows where. No one ever saw or heard from him again. But the mark . . . You see, boys, the mark always returned. Now, *my* mother only had it for a short time while she was pregnant with me, but as soon as I was born, *it* came too . . ."

Papou drags his feet against the ground and slows his swinging. "Listen," he says, "I've carried this mark for my entire life. It has a will of its own. A relentless, brutish will. When it heard the bouzouki for the first time, it made me learn it. It took these fat, clumsy fingers of mine and said, 'If you don't master the bouzouki in one year, I'll cut them all off!' There's something it's been trying to get at for centuries. Bah, who knows, maybe even longer than that! But it can't do it with words. And when I die, it won't stop there. It'll find someone new, someone fresh. It'll keep struggling, willing . . ."

I tighten my grip on my swing.

Mark slows his swinging to its previous tick-tock.

Shaking his head, the old trickster bursts into laughter. "But not yet you dunderheads! You saw it there on my back with your own eyes, didn't you? So, as long as it's there, nothing can ever happen to me . . . Nothing."

And for whatever reason, Papou's repetition of the word "nothing," it's enough to liberate Mark and I from our sullen hex. We ask the old man about other bearers of the birthmark. We ask if it's always been the same shape or if it's ever mutated. We ask if it's a genetic thing—if it's recessive, dominant, or passive aggressive. Mark asks if the birthmark is isolated to the Marakas bloodline.

Sound billows forth from our lungs.

Papou stirs two ponds with one stone.

This happens every time. Every time I libel stories, every time I call them fantasy, lies, useless, caprice, Papou tells one and contradicts me. I doubt there's an ounce of truth in what he just said, and yet I felt something tangible inside of me as he told it. Something kindling. Something coming from nothing. Existence picking itself up from its own bootstraps.

Astronomers—who like this sort of paradox—say that if there's enough matter in the universe, there's a chance it won't die of entropy. Instead, it'll collapse and give birth all over again. But no one knows if there really is enough matter in the universe for this to happen: for the universe to hatch into a phoenix. Because no one's seen this matter; they've only felt it. And who knows, maybe the same rule applies to stories. Maybe it's possible for there to be enough substance inside one story that it'll keep giving birth to itself perpetually, emerging every generation or two in retellings, adaptations, translations, sequels, prequels . . . Then the real mystery wouldn't be that something came from nothing; it would be that something *keeps* coming from nothing. And—even more mysterious—that this something is stamped on Papou's lower back in a birthmark the shape of an exclamation point.

CHAPTER 3

The parcel is a six pound square, thirteen inches on each side. Mark and I know this because we weighed and measured it. It appears similar to any other package one might receive in the mail: a dented box of cardboard riddled with stamps, barcodes, addresses, and tan-colored packing tape. The return address reads:

Catholic Charities of Eastern Virginia
4855 Princess Anne Road
Virginia Beach, VA 23462

Underneath this address is a Korean footnote:

기밀

Mark, being as clueless as I am when it comes to our ancestral tongues, has translated the characters as reading: "Fuck if I know . . ."

These are the files most adoptees request but never receive. These are the files Mark never requested but *has* received. Whether the parcel contains his birthplace, childhood photos, his family tree, or snakes-in-a-can, it's difficult to say without opening it.

I sit on my bed, my back resting against the wall. I ask if they usually mail packages.

"No . . ."

I ask if this is a good thing.

"This is a good thing . . ." Mark echoes in a monotone voice.

As soon as I came home today, Mark was sitting in my parents' kitchen, having tea with Mom. He was wearing his red backpack, the one I haven't seen him use since high school. After we walked upstairs, Mark unzipped his backpack and revealed the mysterious cube inside, dropping it atop my dresser as if its cardboard exterior was scalding his hands. I asked Mark what it was. He collapsed into my blue beanbag chair and replied, "Lost in trans-shit…"

"Let me get this straight," I say, "the adoption agency sent you the package, but you, you never sent them anything that might have prompted the package?"

"No . . ."

"So . . . why would they do that?"

"I don't fucking know . . ."

"Well, fucking guess."

"Someone could be looking for me . . ."

"Like . . ."

"Like a relative. A grandparent, a sibling, a mother . . ."

"Well, isn't that a good thing? Isn't that exciting?"

"Is it?"

"I think so."

"Killjoy, don't take this the wrong way but—"

"But what?"

"Nothing."

"No, say it."

"Stop understanding."

"What? What the fuck does that mean?"

"I need you to stop understanding."

"Then why the hell are you here? What the fuck? Seriously, why bring your problems to me and then say, 'Oh, by the way, you can't help' . . .?"

"I didn't say that—"

"It's what you meant."

"What I meant is that I need you to commiserate with me, to help me, by shutting up *with* me."

"Fine . . ."

Mark sighs. One of his "Stubb" sighs. As if I've gone and punctured the trachea of another man's soul.

I try to get my mind off the box. Mark doesn't want me thinking about it, so why waste my time. Luckily, there's more than one elephant in the room. We're collecting them. The most recent elephant is "The Prophecy." Whenever I get desperate, I pull Delphic Inc.'s papyrus scroll out of the bottom drawer of my desk, slide off the rubber band, and imagine what I might have done with those twenty dollars. It's funny, no one ever talks about how to dispose of dead elephants . . .

To help me interpret the scroll, I've checked out a book from the library titled *Cryptology and the Kabbalah*. What I've gathered so far is that sudden hermetic breakthroughs can be reached through simply changing the direction one is reading. So, instead of reading from left to right, I could try reading the prophecy from right to left. Or vertically. Or diagonally. Or, if I'm feeling adventuresome, I could pair the first letter of each word together, then the second letter of each word, then the third, and so on and so forth until I've scrambled the text completely.

So far, my results—to use a scientific euphemism—are "inconclusive."

The most interesting thing I've discovered is that the second letters of the seventh line add up to spell "El-hoa"—"El" meaning "God" in Hebrew, "Hoa" being a shortened form of the English phrase "Hold your horses!"

The preface to *Cryptology and the Kabbalah* tells a fable about a rabbi and a golem. The rabbi, after countless years of research, stumbles upon the correct pronunciation of the "tetragrammaton," which is just a fancy word for the four letters of God's name: *YHWH*. With this knowledge, the rabbi is given the power of creation. The first thing he does with this power is run outside in the middle of a rainstorm and pile up mud into an anthropomorphic sculpture, inscribing the letters *EMET*—Hebrew for "truth"—in the figure's forehead, and then vocalizing the tetragrammaton, transforming the sculpture into a golem. Elated, the rabbi then asks the golem about the secrets of the universe, secrets which the golem is bound to be truthful about because of the four letters inscribed on its forehead. Unfortunately, the golem, while having life, lacks lungs and vocal cords, so whatever knowledge it possesses is incommunicable. Humbled, drenched, the rabbi kneels and faces heaven, denouncing his erstwhile hubris. He then erases the letter "E" from the golem's forehead, leaving the letters *MET*—Hebrew for "death"—causing the golem to melt back into its previous lumps of unmolded clay. The moral—"*Decryption is blasphemy.*"

"The passport, the one they gave me," Mark says, "the one I came with . . . I don't think it's me."

"What do you mean?"

"It doesn't look like me. The picture . . . The kid's all chubby and shit. Besides, it's not my nose. I know my nose and that's not it."

"Weird . . ."

"Dude, there's so many weird things about the whole experience. Unfortunately, most of what I remember isn't mine. It's second-hand. It's Martha and Ed's. It's not mine."

Of all the years I've known Mark, this is the one topic he never brings up. This is the constant target of his super power: "omission." And the few times I've dared to broach the topic myself, Mark's responded with indifference, as if I was talking about someone else.

"Apparently, I didn't have many possessions," Mark says. "But I guess, I guess that's not a big surprise. Instead of a suitcase, I had like a silver lunch-pail. My slippers, they had wings. I was really into flying apparently—you know, rockets and spaceships and all that. When I got on the plane, they gave me a little toy jet to shut me up. It took Martha a month until she could rip the toy out of my hands. I was like a pit-bull that had locked its jaws and wouldn't let go. I bathed with that fucking jet—I ate with it, I slept with it, I even picked my nose with it . . . And now, I don't even know where it is."

Burrowing his back into my beanbag chair, Mark reclines and tilts his head to face the box. The whites of his eyes are snared in red nets.

I once had a dream about Mark's origins. The dream also involved aviation. I dreamt an infant Mark was being delivered by a postal stork. The shipment was running smoothly until, suddenly, mid-delivery, Mark wakes up, climbs on top of the stork, and slips on a mad bomber hat. He then begins steering the bird like a pilot prodigy, reveling in aerial acrobatics: barrel-rolls, tailslides, hammerheads, and other aviation feats. He does his best to stay afloat for as long as possible, to delay his birth and maximize his potential energy. But the stork—being a bird and not a plane—faints from exhaustion, sending the two plummeting to the ground, where they crash in front of a police station. Touching the gravel with his toes, Mark throws his hat off in disgust and sobs inconsolably.

"Killjoy, you'll get a kick out of this," Mark says, sitting up, shaking his gaze free of the box. "When Martha and Ed first brought me to their house, they used to tuck me in at night in a little twin-sized bed, but they would always find me curled up on the floor in the morning. I'm not sure how long the whole thing lasted, but, for a little while at least, every time they left me on the bed, they'd find me curled up on the floor. I guess the floor felt like home."

"Did you have any problems with American food?"

"No, I don't think so . . . I don't remember . . . W-what do you think my name is?"

"Your name? Uh, didn't you come with a passport? What's on it?"

"It's just something the orphanage made up. It's as real as 'Mark Connor'. But what do you think my *real* name is?"

"What do you mean by 'real' name?"

"What my Mom gave me."

"And what if she didn't give you one?"

"Just fucking pretend she did."

"Okay . . . uh, what's a typical Korean name?"

"You know—Lee, Park, Kim . . ."

"How about Jim Lee."

"Isn't he the old X-Men artist?"

"Yeah."

"Is he Korean?"

"I think so."

"What else?"

"I don't know—what do you think?"

"Why limit ourselves to Korean names? It's not like 'Stubb' is Greek—"

"But that's not my 'real' name . . ."

"Whatever, for all we know, my name could be Nigel Nebuchadnezzar . . ."

"I'd be so jealous."

"What about Prince Mwindo?"

"Royalty?"

"Why not? I could be inbred."

"What about Marcus Cornelius Scipio Asianus?"

"Dude, that would be fucking amazing . . ."

"Mark, what do you think's inside?"

"I don't know—a teddy bear or some shit like that."

"A six pound teddy bear?"

"He could've gotten wet."

"What if it's letters from a relative?"

"Let me get this straight—a six pound teddy bear is out of the question but a six pound stack of letters from some relative who now has carpel tunnel is legit?"

"Fine, you have a point . . ."

"What if it's a cube of infinite power?"

"Always a possibility . . ."

"Killjoy, what do Superman's parents send him from Krypton?"

"In the comics, they don't send him anything. But if you're referring to the movies, his spaceship has a crystal seed inside which later blooms into the Fortress of Solitude."

"I could live with that."

"I could start calling you Kal-El."

"Birds, did you know that when birds are born, they're born with a little buck tooth. It's called an 'egg tooth'. It's only purpose is to help them break free from their egg. I just thought of this, but what if it's something like that: something which will prove useless twenty one years after the fact."

"Then we'll just toss the fucking dentures and be done with it—"

"Do me a favor."

"What?"

"Keep it here. Don't open it. I don't know, just drape it with something." Mark gets up and grabs the green bath towel hanging on my desk chair. He throws it over the box and lulls it to sleep.

"Perfect," he says.

"So, so we're not opening it?"

"Not yet."

"Okay . . ."

"Oh, I almost forgot." Mark digs through his backpack and pulls out a crown. It's the prop Papou used for playing King Priam in *Troy: the True Story*.

"I thought you borrowed this?" I ask.

"I did. But they never asked for it back."

"So, what do you want *me* to do with it?"

"Give it to Papou. Tell him it's for *Troy 2: Priam's Revenge*."

"Okay . . ."

"The old man said he wanted us to start acting like he was immortal, didn't he? So that's what I'm doing. You should get on it."

"So, you're coming back tomorrow and we're opening the box?"

"Probably not. But I'll call you."

Probably not.

Not that I blame Mark. What's on top of my dresser right now is everything he's never wanted. Certainty. The assassin of mystery. The Anti-Christ of possibility. A parcel with the power to confirm whether Mark was or was not raised by wolves, whether Mark was or was not found floating on the Nile, whether Mark was or was not conceived by celebrities, royalty, peasants, swans, yuppies, a golden shower, or the hermaphroditic god of the lost and found . . .

CHAPTER 4

Underneath my bed is the sound of pulleys.

Stretching.

Sliding.

Ticking.

Panting.

Climbing.

I sit up. I look for a weapon. I grab my pillow.

I don't remember having a fit. Maybe I didn't. Or maybe it was just a staring spell: me spacing out, looking like an idiot.

Underneath my bed is the sound of a snap—the echo of a severed cable.

I see a hand.

An arm.

A shoulder.

A man.

Rolling out from underneath my bed is a middle-aged boogeyman. He lies prostrate on my carpet, chest heaving in exhalation—sapped respiration. He has a sharp protruding forehead and a mammoth brown mustache. He wears a gray suit that glistens with rock-dust and snowflakes. Slowly, painstakingly, he rises to his knees and leans against my bed-frame, clutching my mattress like a much-needed summit, a quilted peak.

He whispers, "I can accept this . . ."

I've always been a vivid dreamer.

I've always felt awake during dreams.

Especially on nights after fits.

I peer down from my bed and ask the stranger if he wants a glass of water or something like that.

He says, "Stubb, you don't offer a beverage to someone who's in the middle of accepting a moment for all of eternity."

"Sorry . . ."

The man lets go of my mattress and leans back on the carpet, his hands holding up his body as his legs extend into an outstretched position. Pulling out a metal flask from his blazer, he says, "I accept your apology."

The contents of his flask are chloral hydrate with a teaspoon of Veronal. It's for his migraines and insomnia.

I welcome the day something normal emerges from under my bed. Like a repugnant troll. Or a shaggy brown yeti. Or a tall lanky humanoid with sharp claws, a scorched face, a striped sweater, and a knack for macabre puns. A breath of fresh nightmare.

"Whatever you do," the man says, his eyes pale-blue ions charged to implode, "don't call me Friedrich. I like to avoid any unnecessary Teutonic allusions, if able. Don't you?"

I know this man. He's on my bookshelf. I remember buying three of his works from a used bookstore. Dad viewed my purchase with suspicion. It was someone he had never read before—a name he had thought it best not to enter, like a door at the end of a long winding hallway whose threshold was graffitied with circle-A's and swastikas. But if one had the nerve to disregard these signs and open the door, they were transported to the land of the soap-maker, where those who don't fall learn how to dance—an alien atmosphere of emphatic oxymorons: Healthy danger! Devout skepticism! Blithe pessimism! Fruitful destruction!

"What should I call you then?" I ask.

The man lifts up his mustache so he can take a swig from his flask. A small tattoo adorns his upper lip. It reads: *Amor Fati.*

"Fred," he says, "I can accept Fred . . ."

Staggering to his feet, he stands up and brushes the dirt off his suit. He then peruses my room, inspecting my belongings with gumshoe scrutiny. Pausing at my dresser, he peeks under the green bath towel and examines Mark's box.

Every time Mark and I try to break up with the past, every time we mail it a "Dear John Letter" with no return address, it suddenly appears on our doorstep, a bouquet of rosemary behind its back . . .

When I started my sophomore year at the University of Maryland, I thought I was leaving epilepsy behind. But then, one morning, as I was walking by the agricultural building and looking out on a small field where my favorite sheep "Huey" was grazing, I had a fit. A tonic-clonic. And then another one the next day. And then another one the next week. Inflamed, the present swelled with the past.

And now, the same thing's happening to Mark. It took a little bit longer for the past to catch up, but I guess pursuing tracks over the Pacific is no cakewalk. Regardless, it's finally here, and it's poised to spring into the present like a jack-in-the-box.

Fred accepts Mark's package.

Adjusting the towel, he covers up the box and then turns his attention to the notepad lying on my desk. Thumbing through the pages, he mumbles annotations.

Recently, I've started sketching the Aesop fable known as "The Tortoise and the Eagle." I've completed three copies so far. Maybe I'm running out of material. Maybe I'm just not getting it right. Whatever the reason, I keep returning to this same fable, piddling with minute details in the background. But the basic story is always the same . . .

One day, a tortoise asks an eagle if it'll teach him how to fly. The eagle laughs and tells the tortoise that it doesn't have any wings, that it's too heavy, and that it's not its place to fly. But the tortoise keeps asking the eagle—pleading, beseeching, entreating. Eventually, the eagle gives in and takes the tortoise in its claws and soars high up in the sky where it tells the tortoise that it's pivotal that, when it lets go, that the tortoise stretch out its limbs and flap like never before. The tortoise swears to do just that and then thanks the eagle for all its help. The eagle wishes the tortoise well and then drops it to its death. The moral—*Nature is gravity.*

Fred accepts my doodles.

Rummaging through the drawers of my desk, he pulls out a stainless-steel bracelet.

It's something I haven't worn since middle school. It's my medical alert bracelet. My dog collar, if you will. The idea was that if I had a fit in public, the information engraved—my name, the word "epilepsy," and my parents' phone number—would give direction to distraught bystanders. But the bracelet, it wasn't just a reminder to those around me; it was also a reminder to myself. I had the hardest time believing I *actually* had epilepsy. After all, I had never seen it myself. I had never seen my eyes stare vacuously into space. I had never seen my fingers aimlessly scratch my nose. And when people told me that I had zoned out for 60 seconds, it was like an astronaut being told, upon returning to Earth, that what he thought had been one year had actually been—to those not privy to light speed—20 years. Most peculiar of all, I had never seen myself flail and thrash about the floor. The whole thing felt like a conspiracy. And the only evidence I could muster was my auras, which were as good as fuzzy photographs, ambiguous footprints. And yet everyone I knew wanted me to believe in Bigfoot.

Fred accepts my bracelet.

Turning his attention to Raphael's *Transfiguration*, he analyzes the poster hanging on my wall with the intensity of an art historian. But it doesn't take long before Fred becomes antsy, uncomfortable. Breaking off his investigation, he says, "Your grandfather, he was a carpenter, wasn't he?"

"Who, Papou?"

"The trickster."

"Papou, he's been a lot of things . . . A mechanic, a cook, a salesman . . . But yeah, he was a carpenter too."

"Figures . . ."

"What 'figures'?"

Fred grabs my desk chair and takes a seat. Twisting in psychiatric swivels, he says, "Do you accept this?"

"Accept what?"

"The painting."

"*The Transfiguration*? Like, do I believe that Jesus ascended a mountain and went Super-Saiyan?"

"Super-Saiyan?"

"It's, it's a dorky reference . . ."

"Stubb, I'm not talking about belief. Belief's adulterated acceptance."

"Then what do you mean by accept?"

"That you're willing to wake up to this painting for all time. Ad infinitum. Without bitterness. Without regret. Without resentment. Like the way one accepts a sunrise."

"I, I don't think I understand . . ."

"So, no."

Fred stand up and slides my chair out of the way. He then steps on my mattress as if it's one more stair to be climbed, his boots smearing mud on my bed-sheets, his hands tracing the surface of my ceiling.

"Stubb, do you know what my greatest idea is?"

He pulls out a miniature golden hammer from his blazer and begins tapping the mallet against my ceiling, pressing his ear to the wood at each resounding interval.

"I think so," I say.

"I call it 'The Greatest Weight'."

"It's the one about cyclical time, right?"

Finding a spot he likes, Fred takes out a pencil and draws a circle.

"It goes like this," he says. "Everything's happened before and everything will happen again. The exact same things will happen in the exact same order to the exact same people. Meaning, someday in the future—if you want to call it that—I'll come out from under your bed and we'll do this all over again. And again. And again. And again."

I'm not sure why, but Fred's greatest idea, it reminds me of that old story in the *Arabian Nights*—the one called "The Fisherman and the Genie" . . .

One day, a fisherman catches a rusted jar in his net. He uncorks it and a genie the size of a minaret emerges from the jar. The genie, instead of offering the customary three wishes to his liberator, offers death instead. The fisherman gets down on his knees and pleads with the genie, asking why he, the genie's liberator, deserves death. The genie responds, "After 10 years, I swore to reward my liberator with untold riches. After 100 years, I swore to bestow on my liberator the wisdom of Solomon. After 1,000 years, immortality. Until, finally, having lived an eternity inside that jar, I swore to award my liberator the most blessed gift of all: death."

I can't help but think that if Fred's right, if life really is nothing more than infinite repetition, then what will happen is that we'll all end up sympathizing not with the fisherman, but the genie.

Using his tiny golden mallet, Fred punches a hole through my ceiling.

I ask why his idea is so "great."

He says, "Because of the weight . . ."

Stray wood chips rain down on my hair.

"But what's so great about weight?"

"Simple," he says, "it forces you to mold yourself into something you could stomach for all eternity. It forces you to make your life into a classic—something worth rereading, repeating."

"But what if we're already in the middle of a life we've lived out before? I mean, what if this isn't the first life, the 'blueprint' life; what if this is the eight billionth life, the predetermined life?"

A bluish-black beam seeps into my bedroom through Fred's newly punctured manhole. He stares into the sky, basking in his nocturnal spotlight.

"Why would you accept *that*?" he asks.

"I'm not *accepting* it," I say, "I'm just posing it as a possibility."

Fred accepts the hole in my ceiling.

Putting away his tools, he leaps off my mattress and takes another swig from his flask.

"But a meaningless possibility . . ." he says.

"Look, I'm just saying your thought-experiment has holes in it—"

Fred laughs. He laughs so hard he has to steady himself by leaning one arm against the wall.

"What's so funny?" I ask.

"Stubb, you don't poke holes *in* a thought-experiment; you poke holes *with* a thought-experiment."

"Into what?"

Fred regains his balance. Walking to the middle of my room, he twists around in a circle, a slow 360 showcase of my attic bedroom.

"Cells . . ." he says.

"Cells?"

"Tell me—do you have a greatest idea?"

"No . . ."

"What about all those fables in your notebook?"

Fred returns to my office chair, grabbing it and lifting it on top of my mattress.

I squeeze my legs into my body, making room for the legs of the chair.

I say, "The doodles, they don't really mean anything. I just sort of draw fables every now and then."

"*Scheisse!*"

"What?"

"Stamp some fucking meaning into them! What's wrong with you? Are you expecting the world to come wrapped in a bow of meaning?"

Fred takes another swig from his flask. He steadies my wobbling chair and boards it.

"What about epilepsy?" he says. "What can you do with that?"

"I, I'm not sure . . ."

Fred hoists himself up, lifting his body through the manhole in my ceiling.

"Have you ever heard of SUDEP?" I ask.

Fred's chest fades into the twilight.

"It's short for Sudden Unexpected Death in Epilepsy," I say. "They don't really know what causes it. Some people with epilepsy, they just die randomly in their sleep. Especially young males in their 20's."

Fred kicks his feet for leverage, knocking the chair off my mattress.

His waist disappears.

"I, I could die at any moment," I say.

His boots disappear.

I stand up and yell through the manhole: "Give me an idea to live by!"

Fred reappears, upside down, his head periscoping through the hole in my ceiling.

"You might not wake up tomorrow . . ." he says.

"Will you give me a 'greatest' idea?"

Fred winces. He says, "Stubb, I'm not a crutch . . ." He then lifts his head up and disappears. The footsteps of the 19th century invalid prophet, Friedrich Nietzsche, patter on my roof like a stray cat.

His voice barely audible through the ceiling, he says, "Beware of the curse of the carpenter."

"What's the curse of the carpenter?!" I shout.

"It's endemic to all sons of carpenters."

"But what is it?!"

"Never having to know creation as a vocation."

CHAPTER 5

I'm not sure how my parents found out about last night's fit. When it comes to seizures, it's impossible to tell how much they know. I never see what they see. They never see what I see. Epilepsy is like one of those enchanted mirrors hanging in the walls of myth: those who look in from the outside see one image; those who are trapped inside see another. But they know. Why else would we be here, having dinner, just the three of us on a "spontaneous" night out, my father dilating on famous war speeches of resiliency, scaling an implicit ladder from minor military setbacks to unforeseen seizures; my mother explicating the nuances of horticulture, tacitly drawing a connection from the trials and tribulations of the world's flora to the electric abnormalities of the human brain. This only happens after fits. That's when we venture out to a new restaurant and talk about epilepsy without talking about epilepsy. Because words are invasive pricks.

We're dining at a Hollywood-themed tapas restaurant called "Bobbywood's." I sit back in our corner booth and soak in a barrage of stimuli . . .

There's Mom to my left, her face resting in its natural austerity: high cheekbones and eyes the color of envy. She describes how she and Dad plan on flying to Alabama this weekend to attend her mother's 80th birthday.

There's Dad to my right. The sleeves to his blue button-up shirt are wrinkled and rolled up, ready for action. He clicks his pen like an audible period at the end of each sentence. He tells me how I'll be left in charge of not only my grandparents but also the 100 or so trick-or-treaters who will come knocking this weekend demanding saccharine spoils.

There's our waitress straight ahead, a pale girl with freckles and red hair. She suggests I try either the pork-stuffed arepas or the tuna tartar.

Last but not least, there's Bob on the wall, the restaurant's eponymous mascot. Bob is frescoed throughout the building as various cinematic caricatures. Bob-Hur. Citizen Bob. Dr. Boblove. The Bobfather.

Saturday is Halloween. Papou's been on his best behavior. No more sneaking off and rolling down the ramp that connects the front door to the driveway. No more raiding the kitchen and picking at the ice cream, filling in the spoon-prints with frozen milk. The old man's up to something. This morning, he asked me to rent a jester's outfit from the mall.

Dad takes a sip of his wine. He quotes, "I have not yet begun . . ." and then stops and waits for me to fill in the rest.

I play along. I say: ". . . *to fight*," rounding out the response of the Revolutionary War hero, John Paul Jones, who apparently said those words to a British admiral after the admiral asked his sinking ship if they would be so kind as to surrender.

I ask Dad if John Paul Jones actually won the battle.

He says something about the ship not surviving.

Dad takes out a folded sheet of paper from his back pocket—a replica of the periodic table—and hands it to me. I open it up, pressing the paper against my placemat, using my silverware as paperweights. The chart looks like an incomplete wall: the left and right sides of the rampart are more complete than the center, as if the engineers had run out of elements halfway through and abandoned the project. In the center of each of the individual blocks is two initials. What Dad doesn't need to tell me is that he wants me to fill out the names of the elements on the table as best I can. We've done this before.

Maybe Fred was right . . .

When my father's not quoting famous war speeches of resiliency, he's doing little things like this, preparing me for a moment in the future when a mugger might approach me with a knife and say,

"If you don't tell me what 'Li' stands for in the periodic table, I'm going to cut your balls off, kid . . ."

I butter my slice of bread. Stuffing the warm pumpernickel goodness into my mouth, I take up Dad's pen and tackle the easiest elements first: Hydrogen, Helium, Einsteinium, etc.

Mom takes a break from her botany allusions. She begins telling a story about one of her four brothers: Uncle Victor, the prodigal sibling. Honestly, I'm not even sure if Uncle Victor is a real person or not. He could be some ironically named protagonist my mother invented twenty years ago in order to tell stories about someone who's failed in every capacity of life and therefore someone who can make her son feel better about himself. I imagine Mom employs a similar method of motivation at the plant nursery, building a stepladder of failures to uplift those plants she hopes will grow. Maybe she gossips to late-blooming chrysanthemums about the downfall of Venus Flytraps. Or maybe she huddles near struggling basil plants and comforts their pale-green stems with stories of the plights of bonsai trees.

Mom narrates how Uncle Victor, when he was nine, stole a school bus in order to go joyriding in Birmingham. On this particular joyride, he happened to pass his parents on a two-lane road, causing his mother to make an abrupt U-turn and say to her husband: "Bela, I believe that was your son." The two parents then tailed the school bus until it was eventually pulled over by the police.

I look up from my periodic chart. I ask how Uncle Victor's doing these days.

Mom says, "Waiting tables in Mexico."

I have no idea if she's being serious or not.

"At least it's something different," I say.

"You can be as different as your imagination allows."

I have no idea if she's being ironic or not.

Mom, she's an enigma. Like the sphinx. If Oedipus had approached her, she would have posed an autobiographical riddle:

"*What puts butter in their coffee in the morning, carries a bottle of tabasco sauce in their purse during the day, and makes pizzas with cauliflower crust in the evening?*" Oedipus' only escape would've been to leap off the nearest Theban cliffside—where, no doubt, fate would have broken his fall on his father's head and his mother's lap . . .

I catch my hand daydreaming, drifting into the land of Aesop, doodling an eagle and a tortoise in the margins of the periodic table. I can't stop drawing this same fable, piddling with a slew of inconsequential details—whether the eagle is wearing goggles or sunglasses, whether the tortoise gets impaled on a telephone pole or an icy mountain crag, whether the plummet of the tortoise should be depicted with simple motion lines or a blazing comet tail, whether it's a cloudless sky in the background or overcast with one especially puffy cloud that vaguely resembles an old man in a wheelchair smashing a bouzouki. Regardless, it's always the same story. It's always "The Tortoise and the Eagle." I'm beginning to wonder if diseases can contract diseases: if Aesop rabies can get writer's block . . .

Our waitress returns, balancing our first round of tapas in her hands. We order our second dishes before commencing an obligatory moment of silence, a period of reverent consumption.

I make a note of spilling a few drops of pork grease onto the elements of the periodic table which I have no clue what their initials could mean. It's a move straight out of Mark's playbook . . .

"How to Efface Enigmatic Cubes"
by Mark Tae Connor

Step 1: blot out undesired parallelogram using local resources (e.g. pork grease, green bath towels, etc.)
Step 2: wipe one's hands clean using local resources (e.g. napkins, convenient SCA getaways to North Carolina, etc.)

Dad salts a piece of asparagus and bites in. Chewing, he resumes the motivational quotes. This time, it's Winston Churchill's "Blood, Toil, Tears, and Sweat" speech. Dad recites one line; I deliver the next. Our rhythm is the staccato of improvisation—false starts, pauses, interruptions, ellipses. If nothing else, we succeed at masking the fact that we're working off a script.

I look around at the other tables to make sure no one's watching us. Apparently, just Bob, who hovers over our corner booth in a triptych: Bobfellas, Apocalypse Bob, and Dial B for Bob.

The speech is one of Churchill's first attempts to rouse England's slumbering bulldog. It's verbal shock therapy, in which the prime minister alludes to his favorite theme: topographical tenacity—the willingness to stand one's ground, no matter the ground.

Our waitress returns to our table and refills our waters. I put my head down and concentrate on my food, trying my best to pretend that we're not reciting a Churchill speech over dinner in the form of a dramatic dialogue, that we're not discussing domestic affairs in Marakas Morse code.

Each of Churchill's sentences serves as a jab, a thrust. And yet the result is less inflammatory than inviting. It's an old oratorical parlor trick: stab with the hilt, so the blow arms as it inflicts.

I eventually round the speech off, quoting a line about the necessity to put on blinders in order to attain the tunnel vision of victory.

Dad smiles. It's a half-smile. Like the one he gave in response to my third Aesop fable. The gesture—for whatever reason—feels less mysterious this time around. It's just Dad's way of signaling "acceptance," his way of saying what Fred said explicitly. Everyone seems to need this: a way of venting their acceptance. And maybe Aesop's was fables. There, Aesop was able to let go and accept his resentment, his fear, his jealousy, and his anger in the guise of foxes, wolves, scorpions, and lions. There, he was able to affirm even his failures and sidestep the silent void of nihilism.

I return my attention to the vastly incomplete periodic table pinned between my fork and knife. I make a vain observation. I say, "I bet you Mendeleev's son couldn't even get all the elements correct."

"Perhaps," Mom says.

"Really?"

"Perhaps," she continues, "because all 118 elements weren't discovered yet."

"Well, how about this—when you invent something, I'll remember it."

"Will you?"

"Yeah . . ."

"How about your initials?"

"My initials?"

"Yeah, you know, *that* invention . . ."

"Ah . . ."

"You can start by finding yourself on the periodic chart."

I count two to the left of Einsteinium and jot "Curium"under the letters "Cm." Curium, it's one of those elements you can only create with plutonium and a particle accelerator. It's one of those elements which, to use my mother's favorite phrase: "*Isn't worth the powder to blow itself to hell.*"

One square above Curium and two to the left is "Sm." I suppose these letters could be considered my alternate initials. I jot down the name "Samarium." It's not quite the celebrity that Oxygen or Carbon is, but, as opposed to Curium, at least it exists. I then take my mother's advice regarding imagination and draw an arrow from Samarium to "Xe," Xenon, a noble gas unsuspecting of such subterfuge. From there, I start planning an invasion of "Au," the goldmine of the periodic table.

"All of this would be a little easier," I say "if the chemists who discovered these elements had put a little more thought into the names. I mean, don't get me wrong—the nickname of 'the Noble Gases' is nice and all—but how am I supposed to remember that Neon and Argon are noble? I mean, what's so noble about Neon?"

Dad asks if I would've preferred names like "Gawain" and "Charlemagne."

"Yeah, I mean, even something like 'the Buddha' would've been more helpful. The Buddha, he doesn't need other dudes' electrons. He's empty of desire. He's in Nirvana. If the Buddha was a noble gas, that would totally make sense. Besides, he taught the four *noble* truths—how much more noble can you get?"

"Well, there *is* Thorium," Dad says. "I believe Thorium was named after Thor because of its radioactive tendencies."

"True, but even there they sorta missed the boat. I mean, Thor's powerful and all, but he's not radioactive. He's a god. He was just born that way. Whereas the Hulk, his power actually originates from radioactivity—"

"Some of the histories," Dad says, redirecting the conversation back to the periodic table, "of discovering the elements are actually quite fascinating. Numerous scientists died attempting to isolate Fluorine. It was such a reactive gas that it would instantly try to bond with the human tissues around it, destroying skin, veins, lungs—"

"And that's the kind of story that would've made chemistry so much more exciting in high school."

"True," he says. "Unfortunately, as far as English is concerned, it's hard to convince my students that a poet died discovering metaphors."

Mom laughs.

Dad refills their wine.

I focus back on the periodic table. The elements resemble little toy boxes stacked like Legos in a phonetic sandbox. I imagine all chemists, at some point or another, succumb to the desire to play with these blocks, to take off their safety goggles, discard their data, and simply grab hold of each element with both hands, groping about their individual properties like toddlers with a Rubik's cube. Indulging their inner alchemist. Mom, Dad, they're no different. They're just two more medieval madcaps who think it's possible to morph something shit-stained and shriveled into something luminous, untarnishable. All parents are like this. All parents are alchemists. And I guess the least their offspring can do is play along, humor them: put on a robe, light a Bunsen burner, and leave no philosopher's stone unturned.

CHAPTER 6

Peeking outside through the hallway window, fingers wedged into the blinds, Papou shouts, "Positions! Positions!" Crowned as King Priam, the old man's head radiates royalty. Draped in a purple blanket, his body quivers in majesty. Adorned with rings of aluminum foil, his hands glitter nobility. No longer acting, his eyes shine with imperial intensity.

I give a thumbs-up signal to the figures behind me.

Yiayia and Mark scurry into the shadows.

Placing my hand on the old trickster's shoulder, I tell Papou that we're ready.

Examining my green and yellow jester outfit, my grandfather says, "Every plot needs a fool."

I nod my head, allowing the bells atop my coxcomb to jingle in approval.

As the trick-or-treating outside winds down to a sparse and fragmented looting, Papou and I dim the lights to the hallway and await the last two visitors of the night: a pair of five year-old twins known as "The Sons of Thunder."

The fact that Papou's dressed up like a fairy tale sovereign, the fact that I'm dressed up like that sovereign's fool, the fact that Yiayia and Mark are scurrying into "positions"—all of this is leading up to now: the moment little James and John, our neighbors' sons, come storming up our front steps, demanding chocolate taxes.

The doorbell rings.

Papou grabs the knob to the front door and pauses. He says, "Put on a smile, *Kalo Pathee*. Mischief is polite."

No one really knows how Papou first became enamored with Halloween. Some suggest that the seed was planted in his head by listening to the radio as a toddler; others that it was sowed into his soul as an innate idea by Lucifer; others that he caught wind of the holiday through contact with Irish immigrants while being herded through Ellis Island. In any case, what *is* certain concerning Papou's mysterious infatuation with Halloween is that just two years after the boy had emigrated to the States, his face radiated like an immolated turnip at the thought of bringing the unorthodox festivity of trick-or-treating to the city of Norfolk. And so, on October 31st 1931, at age seven, Papou ventured into an otherwise childless night, armed with a deck of cards, a broom, and his uncle's mandolin on his back, determined to knock on every door in sight and offer up his services for donations, his ditties for alms, and his tricks for treats. And after three years of proselytizing the gospel of Jack, Papou and a handful of likeminded missionaries—aided by some noteworthy press in the city's newspaper—sold the tradition of trick-or-treating to Norfolk's population for the price of a pound of sugar.

Papou opens the front door and greets the Sons of Thunder.

Each member of the vaunted duo is three feet tall, brown-haired, blue-eyed, missing a front tooth, and dressed in Spiderman fatigues. Each signifies the futility of resistance by flaunting their sagging spoils. Behind the two boys stands their parents, Mr. and Mrs. Carney—red eyes and disheveled hair.

Papou and I are given the following option: to either "twick" or "tweet" . . .

Sidestepping the dilemma, Papou tells James and John how we would love to give them candy, but, tragically, all night long, we've been forced to close our doors to tonight's trick-or-treaters because an unknown thief has stolen our royal chocolate-chip cookies.

The old man recites his lines as if they had been hand-delivered by Shakespeare. A forgotten mobility infuses his face.

"*Da, Jo-Jo*?" asks John, the younger spokesperson of the Sons of Thunder.

The question is posed in "twin-speak," a language with a native population of two. Possessing a rudimentary knowledge of the tongue, we're able to deduce that *Jo-Jo* means "Papou" and that *Da* is a flexible linguistic term which can mean practically anything, but in this case probably means "Really?" or "You're not messing with us, are you?" or "You're sure there's no Butterfingers in the pantry, old man?"

"King *Jo-Jo*," Papou says, correcting the two superheroes as he points to his crown.

"King *Jo-Jo* . . ." the twins echo in suspicion.

Waving the heroes inside, Papou pinches the bridge of his nose in palpable grief. He explains how he's been waiting for such a pair to come to his door all night, a heroic pair who can help him in capturing the cookie-stealing culprit.

I take Mr. and Mrs. Carney's coats and hang them up in the hallway closet. Mr. Carney compliments our dedication to the haunted house. Mrs. Carney assures me that she's left her camera at home, despite earlier threats.

I nod, allowing the bells atop my head to jingle in appreciation.

On the same day that my parents and I went out to dinner at Bobbywood's, Yiayia and Papou had gone on a morning stroll. On their way back to the house, they happened to bump into our next door neighbors, Mr. and Mrs. Carney. As the two couples chitchatted, the subject inexorably turned to the Sons of Thunder, who, characteristically, had stolen the cookies atop the refrigerator before their parents had even woken up. Papou asked if Mr. and Mrs. Carney wouldn't mind bringing the boys over on Saturday night for Halloween. The Carneys, intrigued, agreed.

The day the Sons of Thunder were born, Yiayia was teaching Mrs. Carney how to play her favorite card game, *Golga*. After drawing the two of clubs, Mrs. Carney's water broke, initiating what Mark and I like to call "The Stripling Chronicles"—war stories from the front lines of parenting. My favorite of these stories is how James, fourteen months-old, eyed his brother sleeping through the wooden slats of his crib and drew first blood by launching a triceratops mortar across the room and into his brother's crib.

James and John announce to King *Jo-Jo* that they'll help the old man for a reward of four "roy-ill" chocolate-chip cookies.

Papou agrees and claps his hands. He informs the twins that the thief has encaved himself inside this house and that although the way is long and perilous, he can offer them a guide to lead them on their journey. He points a finger in my direction.

The twins turn their attention to me. They laugh. When they've had their fill, they call me a *zallywad* . . .

I refrain from asking Mr. and Mrs. Carney to translate, thinking it best not to know what a *zallywad* is. Instead, I turn to Papou and plead, "Prithee . . ."

But the old man just repeats his line about being able to offer a guide and gestures once again in my direction.

Relenting, I grab the flaps to my skirt and curtsy.

As a parting gift, Papou hands the two heroic mercenaries a plastic bag stuffed with baby carrots. Initially, the Sons of Thunder acknowledge the bag with closed fists. But after explaining at length the carrots' magical properties—the fact that the orange vegetables are "necessary nutrients for dark times" and so on and so forth—Papou is able to convince James, the braver of the two, to claim the dangling bag.

And so the Sons of Thunder and Nuncle the Fool started out on their long journey down King Jo-Jo's unlit hallway as they trail-blazed through a fog of cobwebs in search of the contemptuous thief of the "roy-ill" chocolate-chip cookies . . .

Halfway down the hallway, the twins make the following selfless realization: if they take a few steps back and let me lead the way, the majority of the cobwebs will stick to my costume and not theirs, making their guide not only a *zallywad* but a mummified *zallywad*.

Entangled in what feels like all twenty dollars worth of our store-bought webbing, I reach the door to the sun-porch and look back at the twins for their approval, an approval which they give with the bubbling confidence of all safely-ensconced leaders. I then turn the knob to the door and open it slowly, cautiously, triggering the desired sound: creaking.

Last night, under Papou's orders, Yiayia and I took the door-pins out of their hinges. We then wiped them down with soap and left them in water overnight. This afternoon, we returned the pins to their hinges and tested the outcome. Shaking with delight, Papou listened to the spooky sonic effect as if it were a "door sonata" composed by Mozart.

The sun-porch is covered in darkness, minimally lit by two orange orbs, two electric jack-o-lanterns placed at opposite corners of the room.

The twins follow behind me, one at each leg.

John makes a harrowing discovery. He motions towards the couch—"*Da!!*"

James follows suit, adding what sounds like an ontological speculation to his brother's discovery—"*Ka?!*"

Lying on the couch is Yiayia, fake snoring and wearing a latex devil's mask, a mask whose hornlessness is due to the jerry-rigged scalping job which Papou and I had to perform in order to make room for her natural bough of curly white hair.

I put a finger to my lips.

The Sons of Thunder mimic.

Whispering, I ask, "Do you boys—"

"Men," John corrects.

"Spidermen," James amends.

"King Spidermen," John refines, pointing to his uncrowned head.

"Yes, of course—do, do you King Spidermen know how to sneak?" I say as obsequiously as possible, personifying the verb: tucking my elbows into my hips, hunching my back, and tiptoeing forward.

The twins nod and mimic.

And so it happened that slowly, melodramatically, the Sons of Thunder and Nuncle the Fool snuck past the hornless couch-napping demon and continued on in their quest to find and bring to justice the filcher of the "roy-ill" chocolate-chip cookies . . .

The den's even darker than the sun-porch. The only source of light glows from above, where a string of orange mini-lights are tied to the room's ceiling fan. Hanging down from the fan's only un-illuminated blade is a key drooping from a lanyard.

I rush forward in the darkness and feel my way to the bedroom door. Attempting to turn the knob in vain, I cry: "Alas, King Spidermen, the way to the thief is locked!"

The Sons of Thunder shrug.

"But what ho!" I continue, "What's that key atop yonder fan!"

"The key, the key to the locked door!" John says.

"Perchance!" I encourage, "But if only we could attain such a boon . . ." I then reach for the key to no avail, making a conscious effort not to use my shoulders or tiptoes.

The twins lift their own arms up in desperation, showing me the combined possibilities of shoulder rotation and elbow flexation. Eventually, fed up with this nonsense, James orders me down to my knees, mounts my shoulders piggy-back style, and points me in the direction of the ceiling. There, he slides the lanyard off the fan and lifts the key up in logistical triumph.

And so, thanks to the brains and derring-do of Sir John and Sir James King Spidermen, the riddle of the den was solved and the door to King Jo-Jo's bedroom unlocked, allowing for a final confrontation with the thief of the "roy-ill" chocolate-chip cookies . . .

Yiayia and Papou's bedroom, it's the closest approximation to pitch-black we could achieve. We draped the room's windows with towels and black landscape fabric.

As soon as we enter, I close the door, revealing how dark the bedroom really is.

"*Da?!*" John shouts.

"*No lights?!*" James translates in a moment of rare inclusiveness.

I drape my arms over both twins' shoulders and tell them to recall King *Jo-Jo's* parting gift, the plastic bag of baby carrots. James fumbles for the bag in his pocket and shoves it in my face.

"Wait!" I cry. "Each of you must do this deed for yourself. Each of you must eat a whole carrot in order to overcome this abysmal plight!"

"*Da?*" James asks skeptically.

"It's . . . it's the only way. Watch—' I take a carrot out of the bag and audibly bite into it while reaching my arm upwards, flipping one of the room's light switches on, illuminating a desk lamp aimed at a cookie box.

"The cookies!" the Sons of Thunder shout.

"But where's the thief?" I ask. "Prithee, brave heroes, I'm afraid the only way we'll ever find out is by eating more carrots . . ."

Reluctantly, and with the sort of disgust that only the most icky of substances can inspire, the twins eat one baby carrot apiece.

Acknowledging the sacrifice, I flip the second light switch on and illuminate another desk lamp. This one is aimed to spotlight the edge of my grandparents' bed, where a disembodied face hovers, its chin resting on the mattress while its body kneels in between the wall and the bed-frame. The face is that of a blue alien with bug eyes—Spiderman's deadliest foe, Venom.

When I told one of my coworkers about the theme for our haunted house, he called me illiterate. He said that every noob knows that the Green Goblin is Spiderman's deadliest foe, not Venom. I said "oldest" doesn't equate with "deadliest." He said the Green Goblin is the closest approximation in the Spiderman universe to a personification of Freud's death-drive. I said Venom is the Jungian shadow of Peter Parker. He said the Green Goblin throws "pumpkin bombs" for Christ's sake—how much more Halloween can you get? I said I didn't own a Green Goblin mask.

James crawls on top of my grandparents' mattress. He points his finger at Spiderman's "deadliest foe" and shouts, "*Ee Meemee!*"—"Venom" in twin-speak.

"Waitszz!!" Mark yells in a raspy serpentine voice, "we wonderszz how you knowszz your enemieszz so well but not yourselveszz . . ." Mark contorts his head every other second for dramatic effect.

The Sons of Thunder freeze. They look to me for role-playing help.

Mark drove up from North Carolina last night. After working a five-hour shift at Starbucks in the morning, he arrived at our house for a quick dinner debriefing. An experienced thespian, it didn't take Mark long to soak up his character's motivations, hopes, dreams, foibles, long-term goals, etc.

"Prithee!" I shout in Venom's direction, "what dost thou mean vile fishmonger!"

The twins laugh, despite not knowing what a fishmonger is. They repeat the word like a nursery rhyme refrain: "Fishmonga! Fishmonga! Fishmonga!"

I laugh too.

I have no idea what a fishmonger is.

Mark maintains character. As always. "Fishmongerszz?" he says. "No, we don't knowszz about that, but what we *do* knowszz is that if you wantszz to learn who stoleszz the royal chocolate-chip cookieszz, Spidermenszz, then just look and seeszz for yourselveszz. Openszz the cookie boxzz! The thief—or should I say thieveszz—are inside!"

"Not uh," James says.

"No? Then lookszz, lookszz. See for yourselveszz . . ."

John rushes over and snatches the box. He empties its contents onto the mattress. My old Spiderman keychain tumbles onto the comforter. Johns picks up the keychain.

"Da?"

"Spidermenszz," Mark says, "just because you *could* sneakszz past your parentszz' bedroom, just because you *could* piggy-bag on top of each other to reach above the refrigerator, just because you *could* stealszz the cookieszz, doesn't mean you *should* have, no, we thinkszz notszz . . ."

John plops his head down, blushing a culpable red. He scratches my Spiderman keychain, attempting to erase its silent testimony.

James utters, "*Za?*"—twin-speak for "ethical self-reproachment."

There's momentary sorrow, penitence.

"Spidermenszz, with great power comes great restraint—"

"Responsibility."

"That's what I said, Killjoy—"

"You totally didn't"

"I totally did."

"It's your most important line—it's Uncle Ben's parting advice to Peter Parker—and you fucked it up."

"Language—"

"Shit."

"Dude," Mark says, slipping his mask above his mouth, "you're ruining the scene."

"I, I was just pointing out that *you* had already ruined the scene . . ."

The Sons of Thunder, they break free of their contrite spell. They point their fingers at Mark and accuse him of being a "*Q!*"—a "dissembling bastard." Wasting no time, they leap on top of his head and rip off his mask.

There's screams of pain.

There's unheeded apologies.

There's cries of "Uncle!"

There's cries of "Nuncle!"

And so it was that the Sons of Thunder, after pocketing the evidence of the Spiderman keychain and stuffing in its place the decapitated mask of their most dangerous foe, Venom, showed King Jo-Jo the "true" culprit of the roy-ill chocolate-chip cookies and enjoyed their reward, sharing a crumb here and there for their zallywad guide . . .

Fin.

CHAPTER 7

Halloween's over. Last night, the ghosts of the past were gagged with a lethal dose of glucose: it'll be another year until they stir from their coma. All masks are off. Even the green bath towel on Mark's box. Even the rubber band on my prophecy. Tonight, it's just the present and the future: reality and possibility—the reality that I can't stop doodling Aesop fables, the possibility that my best friend might lose his possibility.

Mark's seated in my beanbag chair. His crimson tunic is tucked into his jeans. Propped on his knees is an unabridged dictionary and the papyrus scroll from Delphic Inc. His neck looks like a scratching post: a collection of red squiggles. Battle scars from Halloween.

I'm lying on my stomach, leafing through two books: *Aesop's Fables* and *Cryptology and the Kabbalah.* Under my right eye is a bruise: a purple crescent. No one escapes the Sons of Thunder unscathed. Nuncles included.

The Exorcist plays on my bedroom TV. Mark rented the DVD this morning. It's near the beginning of the film. The mother of the possessed girl hears something shaking upstairs. Pulling the ladder to the attic down, she investigates, armed with a candle.

I scribble in my notepad—*Seizures in the attic . . . parallel?*

Two dreams led Mark and I to this juncture: one spontaneous, one static.

Mark dreamt he was lying on a mattress, using his box from the adoption agency as a pillow when, all of a sudden, the box transformed into the head of Regan, the possessed girl from *The Exorcist.* Rotating in a 360, Regan opened her mouth and sucked in the contents of Mark's room like an adolescent black hole.

I dreamt of a letter-opener. I was sitting in the kitchen, holding the little knife in my hand, buzzing with expectation. I checked our mailbox. Nothing. I checked it again. Nothing. I checked it a third time. Nothing. Not even a bill.

Mark called me around nine in the morning. He sounded desperate—the way one sounds after being bucked off a nightmare. I probably sounded no different. We exchanged dreams on the phone. Mark told me he was convinced that *The Exorcist* had something to do with his package. I told Mark that I didn't want to become the kind of person whose dreams are so dull that his neurons commit seppuku. "Killjoy," he said, "we're running out of time." Neither of us had to work until the afternoon, so we decided to meet up around eleven, that being the earliest time any rental place near my house opens. Mark insisted we scour *The Exorcist* for clues. His conviction was Ahab[2]—Ahab with an Uzi.

For better or worse, we've opted to yoke our problems together. Individually, they just weren't cutting it. Like a letter-opener but no letter. So the hope is to conflate the two riddles into one and reach comprehension through reduction. We've resolved not to leave my attic bedroom until we've decided on a course of action which will decisively handle, once and for all, not only my Aesop rabies but the issue of Mark's origin.

This kind of thing—decisive immobility—it's worked before. It has precedents. It has a pedigree . . .

See *12 Angry Men.*

See Caesar at the Rubicon.

See the Buddha under the bodhi tree.

On TV, Regan crashes her mother's dinner party by tiptoeing downstairs and wetting her pants, dripping urine on the dining room carpet.

I write in my notepad—*Loss of bladder control . . . parallel?*

"Holy shit," Mark says, "I think I've got something."

"What? What's up?"

"So, in the prophecy, there's a line that reads: *We think it first smart to toss out a small part . . .*"

"Right . . ."

"So, according to the dictionary, the word 'part' comes from a Latin word—*particelle.* And this word—*particelle*—means a tiny bit or a parcel. But if you think about it, what's another name for that box over there?" Mark points to his undraped package, which is still sitting on my dresser where he left it.

"I'm guessing you want me to say the word 'parcel' right now?"

"No—I want you to say 'Holy shit'!"

"Holy shit . . ."

"Jiminy cricket!"

"Jiminy cricket."

"Heavens to fucking Murgatroyd!"

"The parcel . . ."

"We need to exorcise it."

"What?"

"The parcel. That's what the prophecy's talking about—it's the 'part' we need to toss out."

"Toss where?"

Mark shrugs.

"Look—"

"Killjoy," Mark says, his eyes optic sincerity, "we need to abort the demon inside that cube's cardboard uterus. That's what my dream was all about. It's just like the movie. It's just like *The Exorcist* . . ."

On TV, a Greek priest—Damien—is hiding away in his closet bedroom, trying to drink away his depression and sleep off his loss of faith.

I jot down in my notepad—*Glum Greek dude . . . parallel?*

"So," Mark says, "so if the package is the 'part', does that make it the 'weed' too?"

"Maybe . . ."

"Dude, you're not helping."

I rub the spine of *Cryptology and the Kabbalah* for hermetic inspiration. I say, "Well, you didn't send for it—"

"What?"

"The package, it's like a weed in that way. You didn't send for it. It's unwanted, meddling."

"So, it's the weed?"

"Where do you toss a weed?"

"Are there any fables about weeds?"

My obsession with "The Tortoise and the Eagle" has led to the purchase of two more notepads. The idea of turning the fable into a flipbook became irresistibly logical. Unfortunately, I miscalculated on my first attempt and had to scrap the whole notepad. The timing of the story was all off: it was like watching a movie with a schizophrenic frame-speed. Luckily, my second attempt at a flipbook was more successful. It ended up being 52 pages altogether. If you turned the pages just right, a silent film unreeled, telling the story of an eagle who takes a tortoise for a joyride, a joyride which ends with a tortoise-shaped chalk line etched on a mountainside.

Mark moves the dictionary to the carpet and stands up. He raises his fists to the ceiling and stretches. He takes the prophecy from Delphic Inc. and holds it up, pressing it against my skylight.

I ask Mark if he wants me to turn on the light.

He says he's checking for secret messages penned in "solar ink."

"The window blocks UV rays."

Mark drops his hands to his hips. "Whatever," he says, "lunar ink is more popular."

"What if the 'note' is Papou?"

"Note?"

"In the prophecy—"

"Right . . . How so?"

"I'll show you. Pick up a pen."

Mark sinks back in my beanbag chair. He picks up a pen.

"Okay," I say, "now draw an exclamation point."

"Where?"

"I don't know. Do it in the margins of the dictionary."

"It's your dad's dictionary."

"He'll live."

"If you say so . . ." Mark balances the dictionary back on his lap and then turns to a random page. "Okay," he says, "now what?"

"Now, connect the period of the exclamation point to the tally mark above it."

"Okay . . ."

"Now, move to the top of the exclamation point and make a slight downward curve."

"What do you mean?"

"Like a comma or something like that."

"Okay . . ."

"Now, close your eyes and reopen them. What do you see?"

Mark stares, dumbstruck.

"Heavens to fucking Murgatroyd, no?"

Mark nods.

"The exclamation point," I say, "the one on Papou's back, it's a note in disguise. A music note. It's the note we need to 'nourish'. It's why Papou keeps coming up in my doodles. It's why the note is described in the prophecy as 'old'."

"Genius . . ."

On TV, a doctor is telling the mother of Regan that the cause of her daughter's deviant behavior is a temporal lobe lesion.

I jot down in my notepad—*Temporal lobe . . . parallel?*

"Of course, that begs the question," I say, "what 'oat' are we feeding the 'note'? I mean, how are we supposed to 'nourish' Papou? Are we cooking him dinner or something like that? Can *you* cook?"

Mark returns his attention to the dictionary.

I ask about the etymology of oat.

"Already on it . . ."

I close my eyes and resort to stream-of-consciousness: "Oat . . . oatmeal . . . oatmeal raisin cookies . . ."

"Oat," Mark says, "comes from an old word that previously meant oat."

"White chocolate macadamia nut cookies . . ."

"Killjoy?"

"I'm listening."

"What's it called when you spell a word backwards?"

"Uh, 'anagram', I think?"

"Tao—what do you know about Taoism?"

"It's, it's all about flowing and water and shit like that."

"Music flows."

"True . . ."

"Dude, what if the oat is a new bouzouki for Papou? I mean, if you think about it, you weren't just doodling Papou; you were also doodling his bouzouki. And not only that, but his bouzouki getting *smashed.* And that part came true. That happened. His bouzouki's been broken for like three months now. So, what if the oat is really just a roundabout way of saying we need to get Papou a new bouzouki?"

"But, but what if he can't play it anymore?"

"That's not the point. He told us to treat him like he was immortal, so we should buy him a bouzouki that will last for the next 20, 40, 80 years—"

"We'd have to become bouzouki connoisseurs."

"We can do that."

"What if we found one that has something to do with Markos Vamvakaris?"

"Who?"

"It's his favorite bouzouki player."

"What about a replica?"

On TV, Regan is lying face up on a slab of metal, slowly being inserted into the cocoon of a Magnetic Resonance Imaging machine. I was probably no older when I underwent a similar experience, MRIs being a standard procedure for all epilepsy inductees. Just before my head was injected into the machine, I was given the option to select an album to listen to during the MRI. Recognizing a CD from my parents' collection, I chose *Abbey Road.* I remember hearing, twenty minutes in, a distant croon through the thunking and throbbing of the machine and feeling a sudden longing, like Ringo, for a hideaway in which to flee, for an octopus garden under the sea.

Some of the interpretations that Mark and I come up with, they're enough to make an astrologer blush. But Aesop, I think he'd approve. There's an episode in Aesop's biography where he and his master stumble on a headstone with a mysterious inscription etched into the rock—something like "RFSDT." The master asks if Aesop can make heads or tails of the epitaph. Aesop says he can decipher it if his master promises to award him his freedom. The master agrees. Aesop says, "It's an acronym for *R*ight *F*our *S*teps *D*ig *T*reasure." Hearing this, his master pushes him aside, steps to the right, and begins digging with his fingernails. "You stupid fool," he says, "why would I ever free a slave who can make me a rich man?" To which Aesop replies: "*R*apidly *F*lee *S*cene *D*oomed *T*reasure." "What was that?" "Sorry master, I must have read the inscription incorrectly the first time. But now, I'm positive it means *R*apidly *F*lee *S*cene *D*oomed *T*reasure." "W-well," the master says in a panic, "what are we waiting for?!" He rises to his feet and runs for his life. "Wait!" Aesop shouts, trying his best to suppress his laughter, "I, I was mistaken—it actually means *R*esponsibly *F*reeing *S*laves *D*eserves *T*reasure!" But the master had already hightailed it halfway to the marketplace . . .

As for the treasure, who knows if it even existed in the first place. Maybe it was all just Aesop having a bit of fun, pulling his master's leg. Or maybe there really was a sarcophagus of Egyptian jewels waiting to be exhumed six feet under. It's a moot point. The second that Aesop learned how to unlock the word "treasure," the signified became superfluous.

As the movie progresses, Mark and I hit our hermeneutic stride. We interpret the "garden" as my mother's herb garden in my parents' backyard. We decide that what we need to do is play a trick on Papou by planting a new bouzouki inside my mother's herb garden and then have the old man stumble on it unexpectedly. As for *The Exorcist*, we conclude that the best course of action is to visit Georgetown and then toss Mark's box down the famous M-Street staircase in D.C. which is depicted in *The Exorcist*—the one that Satan is chucked down at the very end of the film. But in order to commit this "exorcism," we'll have to become ordained. This, we've decided, can be achieved through visiting a restaurant in Pittsburgh which Mark has wanted to visit for a year now. The restaurant is called the Church Brew Works. It's a century-old church which was recently converted into a brewery. Oddly enough, this fits well with the movie because the majority of the film involves scenes where priests imbibe alcohol. Once beatifically buzzed and thus, for our purposes, ordained, Mark and I will drive to Georgetown the next day and commit the exorcism proper. And, after we've tossed the box down the steps, we'll head home and start planning the logistics of phase two: how to handle the "oat" portion of the prophecy . . .

Like those twins in antiquity, Castor and Pollux, Mark and I splice our fates into one. The story goes that Castor, the mortal brother, died and then went to the nothingness which all mortals descend to. But Pollux, the immortal brother, was unwilling to accept his twin's fate, and so he shared half of his divinity with his sibling, forging their fates anew, creating a destiny which hadn't been prescribed to either in the beginning. On the odd days of the world, the brothers descended into nothingness. On the even days, into somethingness. Likewise, Mark and I, we've decided to weave our fates into one in order to create a thread so distinct from before that even an old manufacturer of fates like Clotho wouldn't know what to make of the frayed mosaic.

CHAPTER 8

The ceiling of the Church Brew Works is an obsidian grid—honeycomb squares of black cypress. The white walls are lined with stained glass icons: bearded men in medieval Technicolor. The church's sanctuary, painted a majestic cobalt-blue, houses an altar of copper tanks teeming with consecrated alcohol. The second half of the Eucharist is complimentary.

After waiting a week and a half—the time needed for Mark and I to find coverage for work—we embarked this morning on a six-hour drive from Newport News to Pittsburgh, arriving at our motel with just enough time to take a nap before "friar-tucking"—a verb coined by Mark to refer to the combined activity of discussing theology and guzzling beer. Following the rubric of *The Exorcist*, our plan is to friar-tuck inside the Church Brewery until each of us feels sufficiently ordained with the holy spirit. At which point, we'll return to our motel, zonk out, and drive to D.C. in the morning with the intention of finding and throwing Mark's box down the M-Street staircase in Georgetown.

Behind Mark is a confessional, a conduit capable of divine service, which now heralds messages from the pews to the kitchen.

Mark takes a sip from his Belgian Monk Dunkel. He's in the middle of telling a story about an ogre named "Sticky-Hair"and a previous incarnation of the Buddha named "Prince Five-Weapons."

In the spirit of pagan hospitality, we've opened our doors to all divinities, be they unkempt satyrs or rarefied abstractions. Any story—canonical, apocryphal—from any creed—orthodox, heretical—is welcome.

Mark narrates how, deep inside a forest path, Prince Five-Weapons threatens Sticky-Hair to repent from his troglodyte lifestyle.

When the ogre refuses, the young prince shoots 50 arrows in his direction, all of which fasten harmlessly to the monster's thick matt of shaggy red hair. Undaunted, Prince Five-Weapons unsheathes his jade-colored sword and swings the mighty blade in the direction of Sticky-Hair. But the attack, once again, clings uselessly to the monster's thick matt of shaggy red hair. The same fate then befalls the prince's ivory spear, his left hand, his right hand, his left leg, his right leg, and his forehead—all accruing to the monster's thick matt of shaggy red hair. The prince, voice muffled, threatens, "Ogre, repent! For if you eat me, you shall face the fifth and most dangerous of my five weapons!" Bemused, Sticky-Hair asks what that weapon could be. Prince Five-Weapons answers, "I have inside of me a thunderbolt more awesome than any flash you've ever witnessed in the sky: if you swallow me, your whole being shall be torn to sunders!" Sticky-Hair, terrified, releases Prince Five-Weapons and engages in a begrudging conversation with the prince, a conversation which results in the ogre's conversion to Buddhism—the fifth and most dangerous of the prince's five weapons . . .

I grab a sourdough roll from the basket at the center of our table. I ask Mark if he's ever noticed how the gods are always provoking people to eat them.

"Maybe they're masochists," Mark says. "I mean, if you think about it, there's bound to be something fucked up with immortals. Eternity is too long to be normal."

"That makes sense—"

"I was talking out of my ass."

"If the gods are all masochists, that would make all the devils sadists by default."

"True . . ." Mark says, grabbing a roll from the basket. "In any event, they taste good."

"Ergo, they exist."

"That's about as convincing of a proof as anyone's going to get."

"Does that mean we're ordained?"

"Soon . . ."

Mark orders a second Belgian beer—a Monastic Trappist Ale.

I continue to nurse my first drink—a Beelzebub Brimstone Stout. I'm not looking to induce any preventable fits.

Conveniently, my birthday landed last week, making our venture to Pittsburgh a legal endeavor. Dad bought me a videotaped college-level course on the Civil War as a gift. It's from a business called the Teaching Company. I watched the first episode last night. It featured a professor leaning on a pulpit, pontificating to an empty classroom about the election of 1860. The setup was right up my alley: I could be there without being there. The gift is my father's way of saying: "Get your ass back to college." He wants me to reenroll for the Spring semester. Just before dropping out, I had decided on History as a major. The subject seemed ambiguous enough. I mean, what's *not* History? Or—given enough time—what *won't* be?

Mark says it's my turn.

The only story I have left is a tale from *Cryptology and the Kabbalah*. It involves two rabbis squabbling over scripture. The first rabbi, outvoted by the majority, rebels. He says, "If I'm right on this issue, then that olive tree behind us will prove it!" And sure enough, the olive tree behind the rabbis leaps 100 yards in the air, confirming the first rabbi's position. The second rabbi, the spokesperson for the majority, scoffs at this miracle. He says, "Who in their right mind would make a decision on Torah based on the leaping ability of olive trees?!" The first rabbi counters, "Fine, but if I'm right on this issue, then let that stream of water over there verify my position!" And sure enough, the water in the stream begins flowing in the opposite direction, corroborating the first rabbi's claim. But the second rabbi scoffs once again: "What possible authority could a stream have in deciding matters of Torah!" The first rabbi, eager to put an end to the dispute, goes all the way to the top and says that if he's right on the issue, then a voice from Heaven will verify his position. And sure enough, God peers down from the heavens and claims that the first rabbi is correct. The second rabbi, undeterred, unrolls his copy of the Torah and quotes the Almighty's words against Him, forcing God into perjury. In response, God bursts into unexpected laughter. He says, "My children, you have defeated me—bless you for having done so!" Astounded, the first rabbi concedes . . .

"So . . ." Mark says, his hand scratching a recent patch of chin stubble, "so God was wrong?"

"Not exactly."

"Not exactly?"

"He was right about being wrong."

"You can be right about being wrong?"

"Sure, why not? I mean, you can dream about being awake, can't you?"

"But then you're not awake—you're dreaming . . ."

"Dude, I just like the idea of a God who can laugh at himself."

"True . . ."

"You know, a God who actually finds his own foibles funny. A God who actually wants His creation to become better than Himself, like a real parent and not some evil stepmother."

Our dinner arrives: a barbecue pork sandwich and a buffalo burger. Mark yoinks my pickle. In retribution, I claim his largest and most golden fry.

Blessed are the filchers.

Mark begins a story about Odin and Thor and how the two Norse gods found themselves lost one day in a land called "Giant-Land." I've heard him tell the story before, but it's been so long that I've forgotten most of the details.

Blessed are the repetitive.

So Odin and Thor are meandering through Giant-Land, Mark narrates, when they encounter the trickster god, Loki, who invites the two inside his mead-hall, eager to test their skills. Odin, upon hearing Loki's challenge, boasts that he can defeat any man his host can muster in a gluttony contest. He's pitted against one of Loki's subjects, a man of lanky emaciated proportions. Each is given a trough of various meat—boar, bear, whale, reindeer—to devour in a specified amount of time. When the allotted time expires, Odin has finished everything but the bones inside his trough, but his challenger has finished everything: bones and trough included. Flabbergasted, Odin has no choice but to acknowledge defeat. Thor then boasts that he can defeat any man of Loki's in a drinking contest. Accepting the challenge, Loki hands Thor an extremely long but extremely skinny drinking horn. He then says that the best of the men in his hall can chug the horn in one swig, the most mediocre in two swigs, and the worst in three. Thor proceeds to quaff like a maelstrom celebrating Mardi Gras. But no matter how much liquid the god of thunder gulps down, he's unable to drain the contents of the horn on his first try. In fact, only a miniscule amount of liquid appears to be drained from the horn at all—just enough to make it possible to carry the cup without spilling it. Thor, enraged, takes two more quaffs from the horn, each time setting it down in a half-drowned stupor. Loki, a smile on his lips, cancels any future games planned for that night, saying that there's no need to see any more of Odin and Thor's "famed" abilities. Embarrassed to the point of violence, Odin commands Loki to allow him to participate in one final challenge. Thor threatens likewise. All too happy to oblige, Loki concedes, pitting one of his housekeepers, an old crone, against Odin in a wrestling match. The king of the gods buckles and is pinned in less than a minute flat by a woman whose face has more wrinkles on it than the oldest mermaid in the sea. Loki then challenges Thor to lift his cat off the ground. After shedding a deluge of sweat, the god of thunder is able to heave the cat's left paw into the air before collapsing in exhaustion. Humiliated, Odin and Thor accept defeat. They gather their belongings and exit Loki's hall, grumbling to their heart's discontent. But just before the two depart Giant-Land forever, Loki—unable to contain himself—confesses his ruse. He tells the two gods that his homeland, Giant-Land, is a place where nothing is as it seems. "For example," he says, "the man who challenged Odin to the eating contest was no ordinary man; it was "Fire," an element more unquenchable than any mortal or god ever could be. Likewise, the horn Thor drank from was connected to the ocean which surrounds the world. In fact, Thor drank so much of the ocean that he created the tides. And the old crone that Odin wrestled was no ordinary housekeeper; she was Old Age. And no one pins Old Age. Lastly, the cat Thor attempted to lift was no ordinary cat; it was Thor's shadow. And no one—however strong—can bench-press their own shadow. After confessing his chimerical machinations, Loki vanishes in a cloud of laughing gas, forcing his brethren to gag at their latest hoodwinking . . .

I take a sip from my stout. I ask Mark if he's sure that's how the story goes.

Mark says, "Dude, you have mustard on your chin."

"Seriously, I remember it being different."

"Cleanliness is next to godliness."

I pick up a napkin and wipe off the mustard.

"Every time I tell that story," Mark says, "I forget some of the details. It's just the way my brain works with storytelling. But I can't stop halfway through and confess that I've drawn a blank. That's how Homer got blinded. So I make up whatever details I'm hazy about and just keep on, as if nothing's happened. Besides, this version's better. The original had more holes in it."

"Holes which you *remember*?"

"I remember the holes."

I shoot Mark a skeptical squint.

"Trust me," he says, "this one's better."

Blessed are the expurgators.

"This might be a stupid question," I say, "but do you think there's anything out there?"

"What—like alien life-forms?"

"No, retard—like a God."

"What about a Loki?"

"Or a Loki . . ."

"Honestly, if there wasn't one in the beginning, I'd say there has to be one by now."

"Pass that by me again . . ."

"Dude, it's just as retarded to argue that God doesn't exist because *we* created him as it is to say that you don't exist because *your parents* created you. Seriously, what's so incompatible about existence and creation?"

"Never thought of it that way . . ."

"Which is no argument against it."

"So, both sides are right? God sort of exists and sort of doesn't . . ."

"Everybody wins."

Blessed are those who want to have their angel-food cake and eat it too.

CHAPTER 9

The primary use of the Georgetown staircase connecting M-Street and Prospect Street is not, as Mark and I had gambled, a public grounds for private exorcisms. Instead, it's a pathway to facilitate pedestrian mobility. Which makes it difficult to launch Mark's parcel down all 75 of the stairwell's warped concrete steps without "exorcising" an innocent bystander. So, for the past eight hours, we've been forced to loiter the Northwest of D.C., waiting for the pedestrians of the city to slip off their footwear and call it a night.

This, this isn't the first time Mark and I have bungled the concept of "purpose." In elementary school, there was the case of Mark's neighbor's fence. Mark and I were certain that this fence's purpose was to be that of a sieged castle, a perpetually-raided outpost—and not, as we later discovered, a buffer-zone seeking to erase the visual residue of communal existence. This mistake was rectified one Saturday morning when Mark and I stormed the fence with an arsenal of pebbles, plastic swords, paper airplanes, hocked loogies, and step-ladders, only to be promptly chastised by a small army of adults for a length of time measuring, subjectively, ten math classes.

Eyes locked and loaded, Mark stands like a gangster at the bottom of *The Exorcist* stairs. He's wearing his green trench coat and black boots. Reaching inside his coat, he flips open his pocket watch and announces, "Ten till." The till refers to midnight, our designated *go* time.

I stand adjacent to Mark, shoveling a carton of pork lo-mein into my mouth. The yellow noodles coat my esophagus in greasy goodness. In between each mouthful, I take a break and blow warm air onto my hands, attempting to ward off the first bitter-cold night of November.

The box is on the ground, in between us. We prevent the parcel from running away by holding it in a "shoe-vice." My right foot applies pressure from the left; Mark's left foot applies pressure from the right.

Georgetown's sky is lit by light pollution. It glows a grayish-black. The stars are blotted out. We can't see them, and they can't see us. Every urban sky is an iron curtain.

In order to kill time and perpetuate yesterday's ordination, we drove up Wisconsin Avenue this afternoon to visit the National Cathedral: flying buttresses, pointed arches, vaulted ceilings, and all. There, we paid homage to a handful of stained glass Americans—Andrew Carnegie, Robert E. Lee, and Stonewall Jackson—perusing each of their stories through a chromatic lens. On the exterior of the cathedral, Mark noticed a peculiar gargoyle: an unorthodox bust hanging from the building's limestone exterior . . .

It was Darth Vader.

The Jedi Prince of Darkness.

The Poster Boy of Asphyxiation.

We must have spent five minutes alone verifying the discovery. When my jaw ungaped, I asked Mark what the fuck Darth Vader was doing protruding out of the United States of America's national church.

He said the force was strong with this building.

We spent the remainder of our time searching for a memorial which Mark recalled visiting as a kid during a rare Connor family road trip. Unfortunately, all Mark could remember was that the monument was near the National Mall and that it depicted Albert Einstein. Parking on Pennsylvania Avenue, we wandered about, orbiting the Washington Monument like wayward tourists, searching for a statue of the man whose name is synonymous with genius. Against Mark's wishes, I eventually broke down and asked for directions from a security guard. We discovered that the monument was hidden away in a grove off Constitution Avenue. There, in front of the National Academy of Sciences, the disheveled old physicist sat with his legs spread out, holding his most famous equation on a sheet of paper. His physique was that of a troll—meaty, clumsy. The bronze of the statue had a permanent crinkle, as if the metal had begun to age. Einstein stared with penetrating aloofness at all those who came to pay their respects, demanding—not unlike the caterpillar from *Alice in Wonderland*—an answer to the question of *who* it was that was standing before him and how much energy their masses harbored. The latter being a quantum way of putting the former.

Mark nods, lifts up his box, and begins his ascent. If one were to walk on all fours, the optical illusion would be that of climbing a ladder to tiered oblivion. Sparse street lights illuminate the incline. Mark pauses every dozen steps, inspecting the surrounding graffiti, reading the words of those who've preceded him.

I remain at the bottom of the stairwell, sandwiched in between a red brick building and a stone monstrosity. Behind me is an abandoned parking lot. Behind that, the Potomac River.

I first met Mark in 1988. He had just transferred elementary schools, jumping ship from Hilton to Hidenwood. Mark was placed in Mrs. Voth's class, despite the fact that he was a year older than everyone else and seemed to have already completed the 3rd grade. He approached me sitting on the edge of an abandoned slide during recess. I was reading *Uncanny X-Men 213* at the time—the best drawn clash of Wolverine and Sabertooth. Mark inquired into my identity. I answered that my name was insignificant because in a few years everyone would be calling me "Sloth Claw." When Mark asked why, I said because my mutant power would soon accompany puberty and that my own gift was going to be the power to morph into a werebear of the sloth variety, my answer being influenced by a recent visit to the zoo in which I had fallen in love with the zoo's lone sloth bear. Mark predicted his power was going to be the ability to "skip" things, such as dentists, speech therapists, spiders, okra, and his father. I admired my soon-to-be best friend immediately. If either of our mutant powers had been the ability to see into the future, we would've substituted my shape-shifting with shaking and added to Mark's list: origins.

Mark reaches the top of *The Exorcist* steps. He pauses, kneels, and caresses the stairwell's cement peak with masonic affection.

A group of carousing college students head my way.

I make a thumbs-down signal to Mark and then do my best to look less creepy. I walk toward M-Street and toss my pork lo-mein into a dumpster.

During the four-hour drive from Pittsburgh to D.C., I made a breakthrough of sorts. I doodled a new ending to "The Tortoise and the Eagle." As Mark merged on I-70, I took out my notepad, fully expecting to draw the same old story: the little tortoise that couldn't. But halfway through, I drew a stork. My mind was somewhere else. It was an accident, but it gave me an idea. So I improvised around it . . .

I drew the tortoise falling and suddenly colliding into a stork midair, clinging to the bird's legs for dear life, forcing the stork to drop its newborn package and plunge earthward in a graveyard spiral, causing the baby to awake from its nap and use its sack to float down, riding a westward gale all the way from Korea to Rome until the infant had descended like a paratrooper through the oculus of the Pantheon . . .

I liked it more than the original.

After finishing all eight of the panels, I put the notepad away and read excerpts from Mark's book, the one his alter-ego puts under his pillow before going to sleep. Apparently, Marcus Cornelius Scipio Asianus is a practitioner of nocturnal osmosis. The book is the stoic version of the bible. It's Marcus Aurelius' *Meditations*. Essentially, it can be summarized in four words: "impressions are not perceptions." In other words, impressions are what the world thrusts upon you—the role you're cast in, the cards you're dealt—whereas perceptions are your interpretations of these events—the way you act out your role, the way you play your cards. So, to take an example, if my house burns down, the impression of this event is simply that of my house oxidizing, releasing heat and light in a self-consuming chain reaction. But my perception is what I place on top of this event. Such as: "My house is burning down *and this will put a damper on my day!*" Or "My house is burning down *and this is the end of the world!*" Or "My house is burning down *and this will help to free me from the shackles of materialism!*" The moral of *The Meditations* is that perceptions are the key to happiness and not impressions. Which is why it places so much emphasis on the careful selection of one's perceptions and the ability of the mind—that squishy pink eraser that God awarded every rational soul at birth—to amend these perceptions.

The students stumble up the steps and disappear.

I return to the stairwell.

Mark does the same.

We give each other the thumbs-up signal.

Mark rocks the box in his arms, chanting something indecipherable, swinging the parcel back and forth the way one cradles an object they're preparing to jettison.

The passage from Mark's copy of *The Meditations* which was circled and underlined:

"If a mark slips through, erase it instantly . . ."

My best guess is that Mark's chanting the mantra which the priests use in the movie when attempting to exorcise the devil out of Regan: "*the power of Christ compels you . . . the power of Christ compels you . . .*"

It's hard to say whether the box will plummet to the bottom of the staircase or whether it will collide with a stork midair . . .

The whole notion of improvising around an accident, it must have come from last night, from watching Mark fib through the forgotten details of his Giant-Land story. Something about the event stuck with me. The naturalness of the deviation. The way a storyteller, in the middle of a mistake, makes a mountain into a molehill . . . Of course, in most cases, the mutation proves vastly inferior to the original and so goes in one ear and out the other.

But every blue moon, one of these improvisations turns out to be so damn catchy that it rings in the audience's ears and deafens the original.

Mark lets go.

The box drops in a perfect parabola. It's combined mass and acceleration are enough to make Galileo smile. Wherever he is—hell or house-arrest.

I move out of the way and let the box tumble past me. I then grab the mangled parcel and toss it into the dumpster. After that, I sprint upstairs and rush to meet Mark at the rendezvous spot: the intersection of 36th and Prospect Street.

In order to make room for a new story, an "accident" is necessary. That said, it doesn't hurt to give the original a push.

PART III

THE BEAR AND THE BUGLE

CHAPTER 1

My first domicile after the crib was the bedroom upstairs. It was a room my father had lined with atlases and mathematic tables. It was a room my mother had decorated with a bamboo tree and a dry erase board for, as she put it, "onslaughts of eccentricity." It was a room which, over the coming years, I would varnish with a thick coating of Marvel and DC comics, using little round balls of blue tack to fasten their plastic sleeves to the walls, smothering all traces of the original beige paint with monthly galleries of comic book cover art. My favorite of these was "Civilian Superdom"—a gallery made up of issues depicting the repercussions of putting on a mask every day. Issues like *Iron Man 172*, which tells the story of how Tony Stark accidentally lights himself on fire after passing out in a drunken stupor with a cigarette dangling from his lips. Or *Green Lantern 85*, which depicts Oliver Queen barging in on his trusty sidekick shooting up heroin in the dark. Or *Fantastic Four 330*, which narrates how Victor Von Doom comes home late one evening after a failed attempt to conquer the world, grabs a pint of ice cream from the freezer, and snuggles up to Machiavelli's *Prince*.

The salient feature of my first domicile: its capacity to induce gawking.

My father would often visit my bedroom a half hour before "lights out." There, he would trace his hands along my 50″×32″ map of the world and populate a random country's contours with history, literature, politics, sociology, zoology, etc. One unassuming empty block of space would suddenly become, under Dad's insistence, a land replete with kings so conservative that they refused to accept even death as a change, protecting their belongings in limestone triangular labyrinths and preserving their bodies in sodium carbonate and baking soda. A second unassuming block would transform into a land which, running low on guillotine receptacles, gave authority to a Corsican piper who dumped half a million heads in the landfill of the Czars.

On Sundays, after church, my grandfather would tell me stories about lands not to be found on 50″×32″ atlases. Lands unknown to even the most cosmopolitan of cartographers. Lands populated by picaresque punsters, daredevil damsels, sphinx-like sages, and three-decker plot twists.

Such were the geographies of my childhood.

My second domicile was the attic. I moved into the "great domestic beyond" the day my parents occupied my bedroom. Yiayia and Papou had come to live with us, causing a chain migration. Collecting my belongings, I mounted the steps at the end of the hallway and emigrated to the attic.

There, I lost touch with all previous geographies.

Sedated on a daily dose of 400 mg of Lamictal and 200 mg of Topamax, I'd lie in bed and space out, listening to bands like Joy Division and The Smiths. Masturbating here and there. Letting my eyes wander off to a tiny character at the bottom right of Raphael's *Transfiguration.*

The salient feature of my second domicile: its capacity for shunning reality and imagination alike.

But this morning, I'm hoping to change all that. I'm hoping to retrace those steps and start again. I've written a new fable. And I think—absurd as it sounds—this new fable has the potential to unlock those geographies of old. Both my father's geography and my grandfather's. Both the ground under one's feet and the sky beyond one's reach. Both forgotten. Both necessary. For a leap is meaningless unless one knows how to walk; walking unbearable without the least possibility of a leap.

The fable—I've typed it up, printed it out, and glued it to my wall . . .

"The Bear and the Bugle"

No one knows how it happened, but it happened: a golden bugle was lodged at the top of an ancient oak tree. What's more, a crow squatted atop this bugle like a feathered dragon. Many animals tried to recover the bugle for themselves—not necessarily because they wanted to play the instrument, but because it was shiny and taboo.

The first to attempt a theft of the bugle was the lion. Claiming its right to royal taxation, the lion demanded to be given what the crow was sitting on. Indignant, the crow refused. So the lion shook the trunk of the oak tree with all its might, attempting to dislodge the bugle from the tree. But this proved fruitless. Exasperated, the lion trudged away, waving one paw in the air: "It's probably out of tune anyways . . ."

The next to attempt a theft of the bugle was the wolf. The wolf, likewise, demanded to be given what the crow was sitting on. Once again, the crow refused. So the wolf howled like a banshee. Howled and howled and howled and howled. The sound was unbearable. Like claws on a chalkboard. But the crow, resilient, endured until the wolf lost its voice, snarled, and moseyed on home, muttering to itself: "It's probably copper anyways . . ."

The bugle became a sore thumb to all covetous beasts. Like a sword in a stone . . .

Until, one day, the bear approached the oak tree. The bear wore an eyepatch. Its nickname was "Bearclops." Some said the bear's eye had been pecked out by a nightingale who had become nervous over the bear's eavesdropping. Others that the bear had voluntarily plucked it out himself in exchange for the guts of a sheep, which it then used for the strings of a lyre. Others that an orchestra conductor had gouged the bear's eye out with a baton for getting too close to his best violinist. In any event, the bear approached the oak tree and announced to the crow: "Never fear!"

"Fear what?" asked the crow.

"Good grief!" said the bear. "You haven't heard?"

"Heard what?"

"That they're coming for the bugle!"

"Who's coming?"

"The king's best woodcutters—they'll be here any minute."

"But, but I have a nest here? What will happen to my eggs?!"

"My friend, that's why I'm here."

"You have a plan?"

"Throw the bugle down to me and I'll intercept the woodcutters and scare them off."

"W-why do you need the bugle to do that?"

"So I can make them think an army is heading their way! Once they hear the bugle and feel the vibrations of me jumping up and down, they'll drop their axes and run for their lives!"

"But what if you're just pulling my leg to get the bugle?"

"Did you hear that?"

"What?"

"Footsteps."

"Humans?"

"I've heard that a human, once it makes a single swing with an ax, just can't stop. That's the way humans are: obsessive."

The crow, hearing this, dropped the bugle and said: "Here, please, take it and scare them off!"

And the bear did just that, skipping off with the bugle and playing as loudly as it could . . . Not that there were any humans to scare off . . . But it was a nice gesture . . .

Now, as you might have guessed, the bear was a jokester, a prankster, a trickster. The sort of animal that would wear an eyepatch even if it had two eyes. As the bear's fame grew in the forest, two boys from a nearby village began tracking the bear, dogging it like fanboy shadows. Amused, the bear took the boys under its snout and instructed them on the foibles of the animal kingdom: the way dogs were obsessed with archaeology; the way snakes were always trying to shed the past; the way humans shaved their fur in self-denial; the way crickets laughed at everything, which is why even the worst jokes elicit chirping . . .

It became a ritual of sorts: the boys sneaking off into the forest, the bear imparting folly.

But in time, the bear grew old. It wobbled instead of walked. It hibernated for two seasons as opposed to one. And it even lost its golden bugle after a close call with a pack of nasty bloodhounds . . .

Until finally, one day, the boys (who were not really boys anymore) led the bear to a familiar spot: a grove with a single oak tree. A white crow sat atop the branches of this oak tree, perching on a silver bugle. The boys had stolen the bugle from a sleeping hunter the night before and had enlisted the crow's help with a payment of earthworms. And even though the new bugle was silver and not gold and the crow's feathers old and white and no longer young and black, the bear felt something well up inside of him like a geyser: the potential energy of the past becoming kinetic, present. Stepping forward, the bear shouted, "Never fear!"

The moral—

But I haven't written it yet. Because I don't think I should. Not until Mark and I have acted out the scene in real life. Not until we've performed the ruse on Papou. Besides, how will the moral get through if there isn't a hole in the page for the moral to crawl through?

CHAPTER 2

Just after work, Dad and I embarked on a mission to solve the circumference of our neighborhood: it's one of those solutions which requires monthly verification. Dad's shirt is untucked, unbuttoned. His sleeves are rolled up. His face: a five o'clock shadow. Every morning, my old man departs our house a dapper instructor and returns a disheveled tramp.

The neighborhood trees are beginning to bud, their scaly brown skeletons sprouting wrinkled clumps of green flesh. It's that time of year again when God rips off his mask and reveals himself as Dr. Frankenstein. The sky is a bowl of blue. It's enough to give the ocean vertigo. The yellow dome of St. Helen's sizzles under the sun. God served sunny-side up.

Still in teacher mode, Dad asks about my homework . . .

For someone not in school, I need a spring break. Mark and I, we only have four days left until "Operation Easter," where the plan is to prod Papou to harvest a Markos Vamvakaris replica bouzouki from my mother's herb garden. Easter seemed like an obvious choice—not just because it has a reputation for regurgitation but because it gave us enough time to save up for the bouzouki. We found the instrument online. It's trichordo—the way Papou likes them. The fingerboard is the color of marble-turquoise. The body has a sandy-brown finish.

Over the last few months, the output of my Aesop rabies has altered from drawing to writing—panels to paragraphs. And who knows, maybe it'll seek out another medium in the months to come. Music? Woodcutting? Dance? "The Bear and the Bugle" is a blueprint of sorts. Reality mapped in fiction. It's how Operation Easter might go in a land far far away if the morals are aligned.

The "homework" Dad's referring to is a little research project he proposed last week. Each of us was to explore a character from Chinese history and then expound on our findings. The logic behind the assignment: once China industrializes, it will dominate the world; ergo, we Americans should get acquainted with the culture of our future overlords.

I chose a man named Zhuge Liang, a 3rd century military tactician known for his clever stratagems during the Three Kingdoms period of China.

Dad asks for an example of Zhuge Liang's wiliness.

"Well, there's an episode," I say, "where his army's depleted of arrows and the enemy is camped nearby on the opposite bank of a river. So, so what Zhuge Liang does is he arms his fleet with straw soldiers and launches a fake attack under the cover of fog. The opposing army, seeing the oncoming boats, ransack them with a hail of arrows. Zhuge Liang then has his fleet pulled back with ropes and orders all arrows to be plucked out of the straw soldiers and wooden planks. He then launches a second attack—a real attack—with an army of reloaded archers."

"I feel like I've heard that trick before," Dad says.

"I'm pretty sure they use it in every movie about Ancient China."

"Such as?"

"I've actually never seen a movie about Ancient China . . ."

Dad laughs.

"Have you?" I ask.

"Well, what about the movie that came out last year—*Crouching Tiger, Hidden Dragon*?"

"Oh, fuck, that's totally him."

"Who?"

"Zhuge Liang. That's his nickname. "Hidden Dragon." Maybe the title's an allusion to him?"

"What made you choose Zhuge Liang in the first place?"

"I don't know—I guess he sounded like someone Papou might like."

"True."

"Maybe a previous incarnation?"

"He does sound like Dad. I hadn't thought about that . . ."

We near the neighborhood pond. Breadcrumbs lay strewn about the ground like a trail leading to a trap. There's a small sign that reads "*Don't Feed the Ducks.*" The pond smells like a cauldron of frogs, algae, and wet fur. If there's a secret ingredient, it's a pinch of putrefaction. Beyond the pond is Dad's "favorite" hill, the one he prefers for its cognitively disarming slope. I try to relax my mind and allow my thoughts to fall into whatever fissure they will . . .

Maybe I chose Zhuge Liang for another reason too. Martial matters have been on my brain ever since I resumed watching the course Dad bought me about the Civil War. I think what interests me most so far is the fact that the generals on both sides were all educated at West Point. They took the same classes. They read the same textbooks. They brownnosed the same teachers. In a way, this made spies negligible. All one had to do to discover the strategy of one's opponent was look inward. Like twins playing chess. At the end of the day, it wasn't experience that mattered but its opposite: imagination—the ability to invade foreign possibilities.

Dad starts talking about a man named Mencius. For our homework assignment, he chose a Confucian philosopher. Dad says, "We can understand a fair amount about Mencius just by looking at his name, which is a Latinized version of *Meng Tzu.*" He goes on to explain that the mere fact that Mencius' name has been Latinized by the West tells us how important he was. "No one," he explains, "goes about translating unless they have a strong desire not just to understand but to own. The simple fact that Western scholars went so far as to translate his name shows us how thorough their desire was to own his ideas."

It's not surprising that Dad chose a Confucian philosopher. All parents are closet Confucians—champions of filial piety.

I ask Dad if I should be able to understand a lot about him by knowing that his name is Alex.

"Technically," he says, "you should be able to assume that I was some sort of protector of men, some sort of bastion of humanity.

At least, that's what the etymology would have you believe. Now, whether that's true or not is another question—"

"So . . . names are worthless at the end of the day?"

"I didn't say that—"

"I know you didn't *say* it, but it's kinda what you implied. Seriously, it seems that all names are good for is making 'Hey you!' less awkward."

"Well, my name tells you what my grandfather's name was. And it also gives you a good indicator as to what my ancestry is."

"And?"

"What more do you want?"

"I don't know—I always felt like names should mean more than that. I always felt like names should tell us something true about the person. I mean, don't you think it would be a good idea to rename people every 10 or 20 years. You know, summon a counsel of relatives, friends, and business associates and then lock them all together in a room until they've come up with the perfect name for the individual in question."

"But what if the individual hasn't changed?"

"Then, then they get to keep their name. They've earned it. There's nothing wrong with that. I just like the idea of meeting someone for the first time and actually knowing something about them by the simple fact that I know their name. Like, if I read an article in the newspaper by a man named 'Paul,' I'd like to assume that this guy was shy, meek, humble—"

"Assuming," Dad qualifies, "that everyone is a scholar of etymologies—"

"Well, everyone *would* be if our names actually meant anything in the first place."

"Yours does."

"That's exactly what I'm talking about—it *did*, but now it doesn't . . ."

Dad's referring to the origin of "Stubb." Originally, I was born Constantine Bela Marakas. Constantine after my paternal grandfather, Papou. Bela after my maternal grandfather, a Hungarian

GI. But after I was born, no one was quite sure what to call me. Constantine's don't suck on pacifiers, and Bela reminded everyone of Bela Lugosi. Bela's suck on blood. So, for the first year of my life, I was called by a handful of hesitant names: "Costa," "Gus," "*Moro*," etc. But everything changed the day I became a biped. It was then that people noticed something peculiar about me: I was a merry klutz. Whenever I took a spill on the ground, I laughed, as if my body had been hardwired in reverse. Everything that should've triggered my tears elicited my merriment instead. Around this time, Dad started calling me "Stubb," the name of the second mate in *Moby Dick*, a man who's defining characteristic is "invulnerable jollity." And for whatever reason, I latched on to this name. I refused to respond to all others, insisting that all relatives and strangers alike address me by my fictional name.

This is the reason why Mark calls his employer my "rival." Starbuck is the first mate in *Moby Dick*. Apparently, if I ever open up a coffee chain, I can rely on at least one employee to jump ship.

Mark's latest venture has been joining the ABANA—the Artist-Blacksmith's Association of North America. He's dead-set on taking his SCA trade to the next level. He's even rehauled his bathroom reading material, substituting *Calvin and Hobbes* and *The Aeneid* for magazines like *Anvil's Ring* and *Hammer's Blow*. For the first time since I've known Mark, he's actually talking about college as a valid option, throwing out terms like a "BA in Mechanical Engineering" and an "MS in Metallurgy."

The familiar barks of Mr. and Mrs. Reeds' mastiffs sound like a neighborhood alarm as Dad and I make a left on Algonquin Drive. Leaning against the hood of a car, a teenage couple shares a cigarette, pinching the three inch stick of paper with deference, nostrils flaring like chimneys.

It wasn't that long ago that Dad and Papou had their own walking ritual. They would leave early in the morning before Dad had to work. Papou would begin each walk practically immobile, his legs in mutiny. He'd squeeze the handles of his walker and muster a sputtering shuffle, the tennis balls on the walker's legs revving like fluorescent wheels. He'd call himself an old Chevy that needed to be warmed up, kick-started.

I ask Dad if he knows anything about the 80s comic book series *Teenage Mutant Ninja Turtles*.

"Little . . ." he says.

"It's not really that important . . . The only reason I bring it up is because it's a good example of this whole name dilemma. The four turtles, they're all named after Italian Renaissance artists—"

"Right, I had forgotten about that. Who names them anyways?"

"A Japanese rat."

"A rat?"

"He's like their father. Not their biological father . . . look, it doesn't matter. The point is that when the turtles grow up, none of them actually fit their original name. For example, Donatello—the turtle, not the artist—he's an inventor and a real brainy character. In other words, he should've been named Leonardo, right? After Da Vinci. But he wasn't. Because that's the way names are: inflexible. Anyways, Raphael—again, the turtle, not the artist—he's a loner and a misanthrope. But if you know anything about the artist, that makes no sense whatsoever. Raphael was the nicest of all the Renaissance dudes. He was the model courtier. So, what would've made a lot more sense was if the turtle Raphael had been named Michelangelo because, apparently, Michelangelo—the artist, not the turtle—was a real brooding dude—"

"But isn't there a problem with your system?"

"What's that?"

"It robs the individual of the ability to add meaning to their name. The name 'Paul' will never have the chance to mean anything else but 'small' because anyone who defies what Paul means will be voted off the island of Paul. Un-Pauled. Names will become mere containers, walls."

"As opposed to . . ."

"Things you can actually add on to. Traditions you can participate in. You have to admit that 'Stubb' is a different name than it was before you were born. And this is true simply because you've accrued new connotations to the word, even if you think these connotations are miniscule."

We reach Mr. and Mrs. Carney's driveway where the Sons of Thunder have expressed themselves in street chalk. To the uninitiated, their artwork is innocent, harmless—nothing more than poorly drawn human shapes. But for those who can read in-between the lines, they see the contortions of homicide outlines.

We make a left and enter our front yard. A horseshoe-shaped driveway leads into a red brick house with a gable roof. A wooden plank connects the concrete to the front porch. Papou's drawbridge.

The first night of Passover is tomorrow. Mark and I, we want to put something on Papou's door in order to be consistent with the biblical theme of Operation Easter. But we have no clue *what* to put on Papou's door. For logistical reasons, lamb's blood was rejected.

I ask Dad if he remembers the old Aesop assignment he gave me five years ago.

He says yes.

"I kinda wrote a new one," I say. "You know, if you're still interested—"

"O-of course. I'd love to take a look. After dinner perhaps?"

"Well, maybe not that soon. I still haven't finished it. There's some touch ups I need to do. Besides, you're kind of a grammatical fascist."

"I prefer to call it grammatical purity."

"Yeah, that doesn't sound fascist . . ."

"How about Easter?"

"What about it?"

"As a deadline."

". . . And what's the late penalty?"

"Stubb, no one asks about a late penalty unless they're planning on facing it."

"I'm just looking for motivation."

"Confess to your mother that you're the one who's been feeding the stray cat . . ."

"You know about that?"
"Indeed."
Mom's allergic to cats.
I've convinced little Zargon that he's ours.
"Easter," I say, "yeah, I can do Easter . . ."

CHAPTER 3

The Closet of Comics is an agoraphobic's dream house: dwarf ceiling, cubicle walking space, and a wallpaper collage of mounted cover art—the latter of these helping to shape my earliest understanding of interior design. My boss, Jorge, is a 65 year-old widower who wears plaid suits and spectacles the thickness of bulletproof. His face is a lunar affair: thin crescent eyebrows, full gray eyes, and half-moon bags underneath. Whenever the front door opens and the greeting bell rings, he doffs his fedora as if subjected in his youth to some chivalric version of Pavlov's dog.

We stand a few feet apart, each of us hunched over and fingering through the Closet of Comics' alphabetized bins, amassing a collection of carefully chosen comics.

It all started a half hour before closing. Greg, Rachel, and Tuan—our high school regulars—had just cleaned up their playing cards and called it a night. The store was empty. Still seated at the gaming table, Jorge and I had decided to play one more round of Magic the Gathering—a card game based on exploiting natural resources in order to fuel the summoning caprice of dueling wizards. I chose a deck made up of elves and indignant trees. Jorge, seeing the green sleeves protecting my cards, asked if I was using the "Tolkien" deck. And that's when it hit me. I knew what Mark and I needed to post on Papou's door. I turned to Jorge. I asked if he had ever heard of the word "eucatastrophe." He said no. I explained that eucatastrophe was a term coined by J.R.R. Tolkien and that it meant "the opposite of a catastrophe—the phenomenon in which cataclysmic events are unimaginably reversed." Jorge nodded. I told him how my best friend and I are looking for an angel of death repellant to smear on my grandfather's door. Jorge nodded. I said,

"Tonight's the second night of Passover, and that means there's still time, right?" "Right," Jorge replied, as if talking about the weather. I asked if he could think of anything better to ward off an angel of death than a eucatastrophe. "Doubtful," he said, his nonchalance in full swing.

Most people think something inside Jorge snapped while working in the 70s as a freelance inker in the comic industry. My guess is that it was the rope binding "striking" to "reality." It must have happened one unsuspecting day while sitting at his desk, outlining an issue of *The House of Secrets*, a comic based on the premise that Adam and Eve's son, Abel, now lives in Kentucky and gives tours of a mysterious mansion, a mansion which is in such perpetual flux that no resident has ever stepped twice in the same room. At that point, he must have paused, looked up from his desk, and thought to himself: *There's nothing "uncanny" except the Uncanny X-Men . . . Nothing "strange" but Doctor Strange . . .*

I asked Jorge if he'd help me find some eucatastrophes. He asked where I planned to find a tangible eucatastrophe. I said, "Here." "Here?" "Yeah, why not? Comic stores, they're like silos of eucatastrophes."

And so, for the past fifteen minutes, we've been digging through the archive bins, uncovering the deaths and inexplicable resurrections of Superman, Jean Grey, the Green Lantern, Lex Luthor, Aunt May, Elektra, Doc Oct, Iron Fist, Magneto, the Green Goblin, Wonder Woman, Professor X, Moon Night, J. Jonah Jameson, and Thunderbolt Ross—eucatastrophes ranging from mistaken prognoses to decoy clones to alien interventions to heart-stopping reanimations. Although, to be fair, we also keep an eye out for less dramatic eucatastrophes, such as the time the muse of tragedy traded roles with the muse of comedy for a much-needed day of gut-wrenching frivolity, or the time the Thing, in spite of his cobbled disfigured exterior and gruff curmudgeon interior, got laid courtesy of She-Hulk's charity.

Every good turn, however domestic, we catalog.

Honestly, I have no idea if any of this is going to make a difference in the end . . .

Substituting lamb's blood for eucatastrophes.

Planting a bouzouki "oat" in my mother's herb garden to nourish Papou's "note."

Curing a case of Aesop rabies with a pot-inspired prophecy.

It all sounds absurd. I know it all sounds absurd. Jorge knows it all sounds absurd. Even Dickens—the poster boy of vicissitudes—could recognize that it all sounds absurd. But I'm tired, so fucking tired, of preparing for the recession, transferring all my funds into some piggy bank labeled "depression." Even if all of these little high jinks amount to nothing more than temporarily lifting Papou's voice out of the faint hole it's been falling into since Christmas, that'll be enough. That'll be something. I'm not dumb. I know how stories end.

Of all things, there's actually a garden scene in Aesop's biography. So maybe we're on the right track after all . . .

One day, Aesop and a philosopher are approached by a gardener who asks them why, even though he waters his crops and tends them with the utmost care, weeds grow faster than anything he plants. The philosopher, knowing that he doesn't know, shrugs and takes refuge in Socratic ignorance—to the detriment of the gardener. But Aesop, as always, tells a story. He says, "There once was a mother with a child from a previous marriage who married a man who also had a child from a previous marriage. The mother's name was 'Earth' and the father's was 'Gardener', and their children couldn't have been more unalike. The mother's child was a brat and a wastrel. The father's—a darling, an angel. But despite the fact that the mother knew just as well as anyone else that her child was a weed, she lavished all of her love and support on her own offspring while shunning and neglecting her stepchild. The moral—*Blood is thicker than fertilizer*." Hearing the story, the gardener thanks Aesop for having relieved his anxiety and awards him a gift of fresh produce.

Jorge slides two more comics on the gaming table. An anonymous work of graffiti is carved in the table's wood: a smiley face with a vampiric bucktooth.

He says, "*Colilla . . .*"

The word is Spanish for "cigarette stub." Like everyone else, Jorge has populated the vacancy of my real name with a moniker of his own.

"Is eucatastrophe in the dictionary?" he asks.

"Not yet."

"Yet?"

"Yeah, you know, it's like baseball. It takes time for some players to get in."

"In?"

"To Cooperstown."

"Ah, so eucatastrophe is Pete Rose."

"He's getting in?"

"It's a possibility."

"I think 'Jedi' got in recently—"

"To Cooperstown?"

"The dictionary."

"Ah."

"Seriously, if Jedi can make it in, eucatastrophe should at least have an outside shot, right?"

"Tell me, *Colilla,* is there a reason that Tolkien created this word?"

"I, I think he thought it was a necessary word. You know, one of those words which, even if they don't exist, *should* exist."

"Like dragons?"

"The word?"

"No, the monster. Dragons should exist."

"They should, shouldn't they?"

"Yes, they've always seemed to me to be a necessary monster."

The gardener in Aesop's biography, he must have known just as well as the philosopher that what Aesop said wasn't "true." But he must have also known what the philosopher didn't: that it was necessary.

I pick up the centennial issue of *Avengers West Coast* and begin scanning its pages, looking for the death of a character named

Mockingbird. But before I can find the scene, my eyes rebel. They refuse to see dialogue anymore. Just empty balloons. Some are thin like lizard tongues. Others resemble long waves of cumulonimbus clouds. Others are bubbles of chewing gum at the threshold of popping. As a child, I imagined we all spewed idiosyncratic dialogue balloons. Before they melted into drool, mine were fireballs.

Jorge lifts *Batman 428* out of the archive bins. The cover depicts Robin, his costume tattered, his nose bloody, his eyes white. The tagline in the corner reads: "Batman was too late."

Jorge asks if this issue counts.

"Yeah, why not?"

"Well, Jason Todd never came back . . ."

Jason Todd is the second person to step up to the Batcave and don Robin's tights.

"Yeah, but Robin did. The individual's not important. They're expendable. As long as the character returns, it's a valid eucatastrophe."

Jorge nods.

"What issue does Drake suit up?" I ask.

Tim Drake is the third person to don the green and yellow tights.

"442."

"I'll get it."

Jorge offers me a handful of comics. At the top of the pile is *Batman 427*. The cover depicts the Caped Crusader and his sidekick standing together—stern, silent, somber—as if holding their breaths in order to prevent the inhalation of an impending disaster. The tagline reads: "Can Robin survive?"

In 1988, DC Comics created a marketing ploy which allowed fans to vote on whether Robin would perish in the next issue of the series. The plotline of *Batman 427* ends with Robin half-beaten to death by the Joker and left in an abandoned warehouse rigged with explosives. Listed on the last page is a 1-900 hotline inviting readers to dial the given number and press 1 for Robin to survive or 2 for Robin to expire.

Jorge asks about my vote.

"I preferred Dick Grayson," I say.

Dick Grayson is the original Robin.

Jorge squints through his glasses like a mole experimenting with vision. He says, "It's true. Jason didn't click with the fans the way Dick did . . ."

"But don't you think the only reason they killed him off in the first place was to set up a eucatastrophe? I mean, I knew—we all knew—that Robin would come back. That was the whole point, right?"

Jorge nods.

"It was all about setting up one more eucatastrophe."

"Perhaps."

"How did you vote?"

"I didn't."

"Oh."

"It was gimmicky."

Jorge looks at the clock. It's time. Five minutes past. I walk over to the gaming table and start packing up our findings in a shoebox.

Outside, the world is black. Dissolved by night. The Closet of Comics alone exists.

I was seven when I first stepped inside this store. After pestering Mom for a month to take me to a place with a selection of comics larger than the breadcrumbs offered at the grocery store, I was dropped off at the Closet of Comics' parking lot and told to be ready in an hour. The one thing I can say about Mom is that she adheres to the golden rule of eccentricity: *"Respect what floats other people's boats as you would have them respect what floats your boat."* Upon opening the front door to the Closet of Comics, I immediately gravitated in rectangular orbits around the archive bins, eyes glued to the walls. It was my first experience of art—that moment when a gong goes off in your soul. In retrospect, the walls appeared to be a collaboration between Jackson Pollock and Andy Warhol. A work titled "Pop Cacophony." Eventually, I rotated my attention from the walls to the bins, maintaining my orbit as I began to cobble a stack of comics the size and shape of Pisa. Each plotline I perused, each chapter I scanned, each turned out to be a story inside of a story that had no intention of ending. I still think that's the beauty of comics: their refusal to end. Even Scheherazade, on the 1002nd night, acquiesced, ended. Exhausted, she lost the courage to say "And then . . ."

When Mom finally returned to the Closet of Comics, it was clear from the look on her face that my tower had exceeded my credit. Luckily, that's when Jorge stepped in. Sensing our predicament, he approached, doffed his hat, and introduced himself. He then led me through my first round of dorky dialectic, a back and forth in which the two of us scrutinized the individual issues comprising the comics I had chosen, appraising their quality with terms like "shared-universe," "bleeds," and "retcon," whittling my once-looming structure down into a manageable bungalow. And this, this became a tradition of ours: me overspending my budget, Jorge balancing it.

We lock up and walk outside. As always, Jorge offers me a ride. As always, I accept. Starting up the car, he asks which eucatastrophes I'm planning to post on my grandfather's wall.

"All of them," I say.

"Will they all fit?"

"I, I guess all of them that will fit. But don't worry, I'll bring them back tomorrow."

"*Colilla*?"

"What?"

"We're going to miss you in the fall."

I finally filled out my reenrollment paperwork. I should be returning to UMD for the Fall semester.

"Yeah, thanks . . . God, I think I was sixteen when I started here. It feels like forever ago. I still don't understand why you hired me."

"Slim pickings."

"Right . . ."

"Plus, I didn't have to pay you overtime."

"Why's that?"

"Because you would be here regardless . . . even if you weren't working."

"Whatever. I was good at what I did."

Jorge nods.

We pull out of the parking lot and make a right on Warwick Street.

Given enough time, all good things will come to an end. The Closet of Comics included. Then again, if there's a drop of validity in the contents of the shoebox sandwiched in between my feet, there's a remote chance that all ends will return in good time to a good thing.

CHAPTER 4

Underneath my bed is the sound of a knock on infinite loop.

Three patient raps. Three patient raps. Three patient raps.

After Jorge dropped me off, I waited for everyone to fall asleep, then I took a ball of blue tack and posted thirteen comics on Yiayia and Papou's bedroom door as quietly as I could. A baker's dozen—just to be safe. Sure, it'll be awkward in the morning, but awkwardness is a small price to pay for peace of mind.

Three patient raps. Three patient raps. Three patient raps.

But then I couldn't get to sleep. I tried everything. Reading. Counting sheep. Masturbating. Visualizing the Sandman bludgeoning me with a sack of chloroform. But nothing worked. I guess I was too full of adrenaline. By the time it was three in the morning, I knew I was going to have a fit.

Three patient raps. Three patient raps. Three patient raps.

I hadn't had one since October. Maybe I didn't take my pills. Maybe I took one but not the other. It's hard to remember having done something if you do it every day. Let alone, twice a day.

Three patient raps. Three patient raps. Three patient raps.

When the aura hit, I grabbed Alexander and curled on the carpet. I don't remember anything else. But I felt like an anchor afterwards. My bed was Mt. Everest, so I slept on the floor.

Three patient raps. Three patient raps. Three patient raps.

"Just open it for Christ's sake!"

"It's locked . . ." The voice under my bed has a British accent.

"It's not locked. How the fuck could it be locked? What could be locked—"

"Don't be a wanker, Stubb. If I say it's locked, it's locked. I mean, Jesus, I'm a fucking boogeyman. I do this all the time. You think I might know when a bed is locked."

Why can't things at least be normal in my dreams . . .

"Stubb?"

"How do I unlock it?"

"Slide the mattress off the bed-frame. And hurry up. It's cold down here. I forgot my coat."

I get up off the floor and lean against my bed, pushing one edge of the mattress to the carpet, making a crevice for the boogeyman to crawl through.

"Are you fat or is that good?"

"Someone woke up on the wrong side of the bed."

"I slept on the floor."

"Everything has a wrong side."

"Are you coming out?"

"Keep your pants on."

A young man ascends from the hole underneath my bed, casual as can be, as if all of this is scheduled. He stands on my carpet, level with me. He's wearing a pair of green overalls which are mottled in red splotches. It's the type of uniform an exterminator might wear if they moonlighted as a butcher. He keeps his head down in concentration as he scribbles something in his clipboard. His hair is light-brown. His eyes, blue-green. His face: pale, rectangular. His name tag—unnecessary. It's Ian Curtis, lead singer of the 80s band Joy Division, a fellow epileptic who hung himself at the age of 23.

Ian takes out a pack of Marlboro Reds from his chest pocket. Motioning to the cigarette dangling from his lips, he says, "You mind?" His voice is not the baritone he performs in.

"N-no, go ahead . . ." I pull up my beanbag chair and take a seat.

Blasé to the fact that he's recently entered my room through a subterranean portal in the dead of night, Ian exhales scattered streams of smoke. He tucks his clipboard under his elbow. He rolls up his sleeves. He checks his watch. He tells me not to worry, that we have time. He stands in front of Raphael's *Transfiguration* and comments that he digs the shade of blue in the painting, describing how he and his wife, when they moved to Macclesfield, decorated his study sky-blue.

"Couch, carpet, curtain, everything," he says, "everything had to be blue. No matter what I wanted to create, I always found it impossible without blue."

I ask what it is we still have time for.

Ian walks back to my bed.

I ask what he plans to create.

Ian kneels down and extracts a variety of props from the crevice under my bed: a folding chair, a hook, a clothesline, a CD, a DVD, and a bottle of liquid. Extinguishing the cigarette on his knee, he opens the DVD case. He says, "Cunts . . . fucking cunts . . ."

"What?"

"It's region two."

"The DVD?"

"It won't work on American players."

"What's the DVD?"

"This is *your* dream Stubb, not mine. Get with the program. I wouldn't dream about myself. That's narcissistic."

"Doesn't everyone dream about themselves?"

"I wouldn't dream about *this*."

"This?"

Ian checks his watch. He says, "Don't worry, there's still time . . ."

He's right. I know what the items are. The DVD is *Stroszek*, which is the movie Ian was watching the night of his death. The liquid inside the bottle is whiskey, which is what Ian was drinking. The folding chair, the hook, and the clothesline are self-explanatory. Technically, the CD should be a copy of Iggy Pop's *The Idiot*, which is what Ian was listening to the night he killed himself, but instead, for whatever reason, it's Stevie Wonder's *Songs in the Key of Life*.

Ian flings the DVD across the room. "Whatever," he says, "this isn't what you would call an exact science."

Bugaboology is apparently a soft science.

Ian opens the case to *Songs in the Key of Life*. "What about CD players?" he asks. "There's not that region-coding bullshit with CD players, is there?"

"No, I don't think so."

Ian drops disc one into my hands and tells me to play it. He says, "And don't skip any tracks. I hate it when people skip tracks. It's not okay to skip chapters, so why would it be okay to skip tracks?"

I sit up, plug in my boombox, and slide the CD in. I say, "I thought you were listening to *The Idiot* the night you killed yourself?"

Unfolding his chair, Ian sits down and begins tying the clothesline into a noose. "It was morning," he says.

"What?"

"I offed myself in the morning."

A chorus of melodic *oooohh's* blares out of the speakers.

Ian takes a swig of whiskey. He says, "Green leaves buffeted against a blue sky."

Stevie Wonder urges his audience that love's in need of love today . . .

"Birds," Ian says, "they warbled, chirped, trilled, twat. But you're right—it was *The Idiot*."

"Then what's up with Stevie Wonder?"

"For tonight's purposes, this album works better."

I ask Ian if I can broach a personal question.

"Shoot."

I return to my beanbag chair. I ask if his listening to *The Idiot* on the night he killed himself was some sort of allusion to Dostoevsky's novel of the same title, which deals with the life and failure of a tragic epileptic protagonist named Myshkin.

Ian calls me a daft cunt.

"Stubb," he says, "what we're doing tonight has nothing to do with the mind. Otherwise, Hamlet would have grown a codpiece and done likewise." He climbs his folding chair and starts screwing the hook into my ceiling. "But to answer your question," he says, "the reason I chose *The Idiot* was simple: I was into Iggy and Bowie's Berlin collaborations at the time—*Low, Heroes* . . . that shit."

"Do you do this often?"

Ian laughs.

I never considered the possibility of Ian laughing.

He says, "All the time. The boogeyman business is a booming industry. Even the dead have to make a living."

He returns to screwing the hook into my ceiling. He says, "Stubb, you're not crazy. Everyone has unwanted wankers seeping into their bedrooms at night. And if they don't come out from under the bed, it's the closet or the window or the sock drawer or the air vent—"

"So why doesn't anyone talk about it?"

"What could be more private than what leaks out of your bedroom's orifices? Besides, they do. Every once in a while, some bigmouth slips up and mentions it obliquely. Like Dickens in *A Christmas Carol*."

Stevie Wonder implores his audience to quit procrastinating and start contributing to the Gross National Love . . .

Ian steps down. He takes a seat and lights another Marlboro.

"You're mad," he says.

"What?"

"You're mad you had a fit."

"How did you know that?"

"There's no secrets when you're dead. That's the worst part. Everything's transparent."

"You can read my thoughts?"

Ian blows a blue smoke ring. It floats up and travels through the clothesline noose above his head. He says, "Stubb, not every cycle can be broken."

"So, so I'm going to have fits for the rest of my life?"

"I didn't say that."

"And yet . . ."

"It's a possibility."

"I can't do this for the rest of my life—there's no way I can fucking do this for the rest of my life . . ."

Ian laughs. He looks down at his props. He says, "You'll be amazed at what you can do for the rest of your death."

"Why are you here?"

"One of the first things you notice when you die is how cyclical it all is. You stop seeing 'John' and 'Jane' and you start seeing bullseyes instead. It sounds weird at first, but you get used to it. You get used to seeing John become John because he hits John over and over and over again. After all, if John were to miss his target, we wouldn't recognize him anymore."

Stevie Wonder recommends to his audience that they have a talk with God . . .

"Stubb, more than anything else, we're rings of concentric cycles."

Ian inspects the noose dangling above his head and takes another swig. He says, "And when you die, your cycles become fixed. That's what death is: the crystallization of character."

"So . . . it's just one fucking cycle after the next? Fred was right . . ."

"You're not listening to me. The cycles aren't fixed. Most are negotiable. But they become more rigid with each year and then they lock in place when you die. You see, it's not impossible for John to hit a new bullseye. All it entails is the death of 'John'. But for every cycle, there's a cycle of how you deal with that cycle. So, there's not just the cycle of epilepsy that makes Stubb 'Stubb', but there's also the cycle of how Stubb deals with his epilepsy that makes Stubb 'Stubb'."

"Can I ask you a stupid question?"

"Shoot."

"Do you know about Mark's book?"

"*The Meditations.*"

"How did you know that?"

"Everything becomes transparent."

"This all sounds like a chapter from that book. Are you one of those people who sleep with *The Meditations* under your pillow?"

"The dead don't have time to sleep."

"Do you still have fits?"

Ian looks at his watch. He rubs his cigarette out on his knee. He says, "We're running out of time . . ."

"Whatever you're going to do—"

"No need to warm up," he says, taking one last swig of his whiskey. "I'm always in character." He sits up, hands me his clipboard, and says, "Don't fill it out until after the show. Then, when you're done, drop it into the crevice under your bed." He stands on top of his folding chair and puts his head through the noose. He says, "Oh, I almost forgot, I liked your moral. Consider this an homage—"

"But I haven't come up with the moral yet?"

"Everything's transparent."

"You don't have to do this—"

"The cycles become fixed."

Ian leaps off his chair.

The whole thing plays out like a ten-minute fit. A grand mal seizure.

Ian's cheeks, lips, nose, ears, forehead, and hands—they all become blue.

The fifth track to *Songs in the Key of Life* is a celebratory flourish of trumpets and saxophones. Stevie Wonder latches on to a catchy refrain and proceeds to repeat it over and over and over again. I lean down and pick up the CD case. The album's cover art depicts a face framed in concentric circles. The face is roughly sketched and the circles are wavy, tattered. The picture resembles a bullseye, but the target is shifting, incomplete.

I look down and examine Ian's clipboard.

It's a survey . . .

Check the box which most applies to your boogeyman experience:

- ☐ *I loved it. I think I'll hang myself as well.*
- ☐ *I hated it. The whole thing made no sense.*
- ☐ *I found it boring. My boogeyman was just going through the motions.*
- ☐ *I understood. Some cycles are dead ends.*

I check the last box and sign my name. The back of the clipboard is bloody. I drop it into the crevice under my bed. My palms are the color of lamb-red.

CHAPTER 5

Operation Easter's underway. Mark and I have positioned Papou on the middle swing so that his back is facing the herb garden. Rocking in our assigned seats, we bookend the old man. Mark's waiting for me to twist my baseball cap backwards, which is the signal for him to reach into his jeans and speed-dial Yiayia, which is my grandmother's signal to sneak outside and plant the bouzouki in Mom's herb garden. I also wait for a signal. A word, a gesture, a silence—it's hard to say exactly what. But it'll come from Papou. Because that way—unbeknownst to the old trickster—he'll have initiated his own hoodwinking.

Papou pivots back and forth, dragging his toes in the dirt. He cranes his neck forward and inspects the grass below his paunch. Wearing his Jolly Roger bandanna and a yellow polo, the old man quivers with the dandelions in sunny solidarity. His face is erosion: fissures and ravines. But there's life underneath. Because impish waters run deep.

Mark rocks his swing with a sudden jolt, like a fish chucked back into the ocean. No longer labeled, measured, or caged, he's free to follow whatever school he fancies. Dressed in a white t-shirt, jeans, and authentic Roman sandals, Mark basks in the balm of a blank slate. And if any more unsolicited packages should come his way, he can count on at least one accomplice. Because even foundlings have a right to be un-found.

I swing like a rookie, full of uncharted expectation. I'm wearing my orange *Fantastic Four* "It's Clobberin' Time!!" t-shirt. I attempt to harness the Thing inside me: that part of one's being which, when push comes to shove, clobbers. Whether it's adrenaline, the heart, or some ethereal homunculus within called the "soul" is arbitrary. Because clobberin' is all.

And who knows, this could be the beginning of a new cycle. Ian Curtis could get a commission for Friday night's successful boogeyman session, while Mark and I could stop betraying Papou's legacy and finally prove to ourselves—if no one else—that the old man's taking us under his wing wasn't in vain. Because no disciple wants to be Judas. Especially Judas.

Outside, the sky and vegetation compete for our attention, flashing their goods, concealing their mystery. Nature's standard striptease.

The sky unveils a plump menagerie of clouds resembling every animal imaginable—both those that made it aboard Noah's ark and those that didn't. Blue and purple hues mount a rich backdrop as an orange eye peeks out from behind the curtain.

Undeterred, the flora of the world mounts its own burlesque, flashing the serrated jade of oak leaves, the pink concentric petals of begonia, the auburn compound eye of sunflowers, and the bristling ash-colored orbs of dandelion clocks.

Put simply, it's one of those days where being indoors is stupid.

Mark asks Papou if humans possess freewill.

The old man clears his throat. His voice is soft, distant, dampened. He says, "Boys, didn't you know, we're all determined by freewill."

And maybe this is the secret of all gurus who grow old but are still expected to spout incessant sagacity: they seek refuge in paradoxes, in bones that'll take decades to gnaw.

I swoop down and pluck my coffee out of the grass, spilling a few lukewarm drops on my wrist. I ask Papou if he ever had a midlife crisis.

"Bah," he says, "that stuff's for dunderheads." He pauses, clears his throat. "Aging, she's not sneaky, *Kalo Pathee.* She's not greedy either. She just takes what she needs."

"Wait," Mark interrupts, "Aging's a woman?"

"Who else?"

"Well, couldn't it be like an old man—someone like Father Time."

"Aging has grace. If Aging was a man, we'd all be dead."

Mark laughs.

"Anyways, so Aging," Papou says, "she mugs us every day. She says, 'Hey, babycakes, let me see your wallet.' And then she takes a dollar, blows a kiss, and skedaddles. Now, the kind of people who have a midlife crisis are the kind of people who never look in their wallets. One day, they decide to peek inside and what do they see—a 100 dollars are missing! And so they lose their heads. And then to cover up this loss, they pretend they're richer than they ever were." Papou takes a breather. He kicks the earth for momentum. The earth kicks back. He says, "Boys, if someone was to tell me that I was going to lose thousands and thousands of dollars, I'd say, 'That's unfair!' I'd say, 'There's no justice!' I'd demand to speak with the manager. But that's not how it plays out. No, not at all. What happens is that you look inside your wallet one day and you see that a dollar's missing. You shrug and suspect your wife. Then, the next day, the same thing happens. You say to yourself, 'Eh, maybe I never had that dollar to begin with. Who can say? Don't be a dunce. You're no Rockefeller. You never were.' Until, finally, you look inside your wallet and you only see two dollars left. At that point, you say to yourself, 'Well, of course you only have two dollars left—you only had three yesterday!' "

And I guess—if all goes according to plan—maybe today's ruse will add a few dollars to Papou's wallet. The ruse is a long time coming. Payback ten years tardy. Its origin can be traced back to the months following my diagnosis of epilepsy. More than ever, I was wont to shut myself off, hide in my room, and pull the covers over my face in a desperate attempt at incubation. I hoped to transform into something else as quickly as I had transformed into what I was. In the meantime, I shared Humpty Dumpty's suspicion that coming down was a precarious endeavor, one which would result—despite all the king's neurologists—in irreparable disaster. But during these same few months, Papou was hard at work orchestrating a different sort of transformation. He had spoken to my father and learned that we were reading about epileptic generals of antiquity. With that in mind, the old trickster had begun forging a wooden arsenal in his garage which he planned to use to lure me out of self-exile. The first of Papou's artifacts was a wooden shield. I opened my bedroom door and there it was: a giant shucked turtle shell lying in the hallway upstairs. Upon closer inspection, I discovered that it was a shield and that it was outfitted with two leather handles for my forearm to slide through. I asked my parents if they knew anything about the shield, but they played indifferent, as if bucklers magically appearing in the middle of the upstairs hallway was—at best—prosaic. So I waited for Yiayia and Papou's next visit and cornered the old carpenter, asking him if he knew anything about wooden shields materializing in hallways. Papou feigned intrigue. He told me to bring the shield downstairs. He said things like this weren't meant to be taken lightly. Relieved that someone was finally taking me seriously, I rushed upstairs, lugged the item down, and heaved it atop the kitchen table. Papou, he caressed the buckler's sanded concavity. He oohed. He aahed. He mumbled indecipherable appraisals. And then, finally, he whispered into my ear, "By the gods, *Kalo Pathee*—this shield is by the gods . . ."

A week later, a wooden helmet appeared at the top of the stairs.

And then a wooden sword smack in the middle of the staircase.

The news of each item was received by my parents with similar indifference, while all Papou could do to alleviate my confusion was to whisper the same words: "By the gods, *Kalo Pathee*—by the gods . . ." But I wasn't that naive. I knew it wasn't "by the gods." I just didn't know *who* it was by. And I sure as hell didn't know *why*.

I played right into Papou's hands. A desire took root in my spleen to put these "divine" artifacts to good use, to drag them outside and imitate those people in history who weren't so different from me: Alexander, Caesar, and Hannibal.

Unfortunately, little remains of the original artifacts. Mark and

I hacked most of them to pieces while warding off the ogres that used to congregate in my parents' backyard. But the hilt to the sword still remains tucked away in the top drawer of my dresser—a loyal shard hibernating after slews of slaughter.

To this day, Papou's never admitted to orchestrating the ruse, despite the fact that Mom, Dad, and Yiayia have all ratted him out on multiple occasions. Whenever he's interrogated about the matter, he just whispers, "By the gods . . ." Like a magician pleading the fifth.

Mark asks Papou if a tree falling in an empty forest makes a sound.

Papou glides his hands up and down the ropes to his swing. He says, "Depends . . ."

"On what?"

"Did it trip?"

"S-sure."

"Then, no. It wouldn't want to call attention to itself."

Mark and I, in order to mirror that celebrated prank ten years ago, we've planted various items throughout the house, items which Papou over the last week has stumbled on during his daily routine. We wrapped a bouzouki auto-tuner inside one of his Jolly Roger bandannas. We hid a binder of Markos Vamvakaris sheet-music under his pillow. We put a cherrywood pick on top of the pecan ice cream in the freezer. And we did it all with the complicity of Mom, Dad, and Yiayia, so that they would respond to the old man's curiosity as they had responded to mine.

Mark and I keep at it. We hurl more questions at Papou. It's not that we're skeptical or dim or ungrateful; it's that answers are as nourishing as lunch.

I ask Papou about the meaning of life.

The old man clears his throat. He makes a brief indecipherable sound before changing communication tactics. He begins a game of charades in which he tries to sign what's never been said. But after a few fumbling gesticulations—a karate chop, pattycake, face-masking—he's gagged by laughter.

We give Papou plenty of time to recover, but each time he begins anew, he's impeded by the same culprit within.

This isn't the first time my grandfather's been unable to finish a joke. Amongst the Marakas family, there's a saying that goes: "At least the secret of the hushpuppies is safe . . ." The saying refers to a day when Papou was working alone inside his cousin's auto-shop and a joke ripped through his brain like a comic-boom. Not having anyone to share the joke with, Papou—eyes darting in escalating fear—rolled himself out from underneath the vehicle he was working on and shot down the street in search of his wife, overalls dripping in grease, hands gripping his wrench, brow furrowed against forgetting in a thought-vice. But when the old trickster finally reached Yiayia—who was working at Woolworth's at the time—Papou couldn't get the joke out. He was like Archimedes draped in his bath towel but gagging on his own eureka. All Papou could do was repeat: "Cia, you ever wonder why they call 'em *hushpuppies*?" before erupting in asphyxiating laughter, laughter which would end with Papou lying half-dead on the floor and desperately regulating his breath. Yiayia, after witnessing three repeat performances and getting the evil eye from her manager, forbade her husband from ever attempting to tell the hushpuppies joke again. And it's been that way ever since—whenever Papou deems it a good idea to break Yiayia's prohibition, he half-kills himself with hilarity but never quite divulges the etymology of those deep-fried corn dough balls. Archimedes, he was just lucky that displacement wasn't funny.

I can't think of a better signal than Papou's laughter. I spill out the remainder of my coffee and twist my baseball cap around.

Mark reaches into his pocket.

"Papou," I say, "remember when I found all those wooden weapons up and down the staircase?"

The old man bobs his head. His eyes widen with memory. He says, "The mystery, it was never solved, was it?"

"No, but I think it's happening again . . ."

I stop my swinging and turn around.

Mark does the same.

Papou follows suit.

Garlanded with basil, parsley, and sage, a budding bouzouki blooms. Yiayia holds the neck of the guitar with both hands. She says, "Surprise!"

I say, "It's a Markos Vamvakaris replica."

Mark adds, "It's trichordo—the way you like them."

But Papou, he can only clear his throat and whisper, "By the gods . . ."

The moral—*Be a pulley, however absurd.*

CHAPTER 6

According to the Eastern gospel of Christianity, today—and not last Sunday—is Easter. And who knows, maybe they have an insider's perspective on this one, being children of the *rising* sun. In any event, there's an ongoing dispute in Christianity over when Easter should land. The Catholic Church swears by Pope Gregory's calendar; the Greek Orthodox Church hails Caesar's calendar.

Regardless, it's Easter again.

For those who hit snooze on the first resurrection.

For those who bloom late.

For those who think one eucatastrophe just doesn't cut it anymore.

My parents are playing host to pirates like those Sundays of old. Relatives from Norfolk and Winchester have docked at our house to celebrate Easter Sunday with a waning Papou. Not that it's a perfect repetition. Not that it's the past verbatim. Many of the pirates bustling about our house today aren't the ones I remember from my childhood. Some of the older scallywags have been buried like treasure, while others can't rough the waves anymore. But new crewmembers have taken their place, and they're doing their best to keep the ship on course. Sons and daughters have started families of their own, and toddlers now wobble about the deck. And where they wobble, the deck is young.

It's already two o'clock. A thunderstorm seems inevitable. A sporadic breeze gushes through the air, changing direction every few seconds, blowing in and out, as if the world were resuming respiration. Relatives wander outside, grabbing sodas and beer from the coolers in order to slake their hunger with thirst. Some toss a football around. Others dally about the swing-set. Others sit in folding chairs and appoint themselves color-commentators of the world. Mom's busy flipping *souvlaki* on the grill, warding off scavengers with her tongs, snapping like a cornered crab. Even those who got a late breakfast are beginning to feel the rumbles of the insatiable god within.

But "Lunch *is* coming!" the cooks protest.

"It'll be here any minute!"

"It's arrival is imminent!"

Myself, I'm beginning to wonder if it carpooled with Godot . . .

I'm on a mission from Yiayia to get a centerpiece for the table. I've been told to walk over to Mr. and Mrs. Carney's backyard and pick out a bouquet of azaleas. I asked Yiayia if I should knock and alert our neighbors that I'll be snooping around their backyard, but Yiayia assured me that she's already called and told them. In an ominous voice, she said, "They know . . ."

A ginkgo tree towers in the middle of the Carney's backyard. Its leaves are shaped like Japanese fans. I remember being told by Mrs. Carney that the ginkgo's genus is as old as the dinosaurs. Apparently, that's why they take so long to grow. They've seen ages, eras, eons. We wear watches which can count to twelve.

Before I reach the azaleas, I hear the opening of a sliding door . . .

"Da?!!"

"Ta?!!"

Wielding plastic lightsabers, the Sons of Thunder stand ready to pounce like Jedi guard dogs. They glower and punish the air with their blades. Both lightsabers are Vader-red, which is what one would expect from a pair of "Cainlets"—a set of twins where *both* are the evil one.

I ask the boys if they want to assist me in collecting azaleas.

They ignore my question and bum-rush.

"Whoa! Whoa! Whoa!"

They pause.

"Be warned—if you strike me down, I'll become more powerful than you can possibly imagine . . ."

They call my bluff and start swinging at my knees, elbows, chest, kidneys.

Tumbling to the grass, I shield my face and say, "I give! I give!" hoping they'll show mercy, but all this does is fan the flames.

"Huey, Dewey!" a voice calls out, "why don't you pick on someone your own size . . ."

It's Mark. Thank God. He's armed with a stick.

High on inflated courage, James and John clutch their light-sabers and charge their latest victim, but Mark parries, counters, and disarms them both with a few flicks of his wrist, sending the Sons of Thunder yelping in retreat like declawed hyenas.

Mark helps me up. He looks over his shoulder. He says, "They'll be back." He then hands me a hard-boiled egg painted black and white with the design of the Jolly Roger. The egg has been saturated overnight with fluoride in an attempt to strengthen its outer shell. It's for today's festivities . . .

Don't ask me why, but it's a Greek Easter tradition to be armed with a dyed hard-boiled egg just before saying grace. At that point, one is obliged to face one's neighbor and "clash eggs." Whoever's eggshell cracks first is eliminated from the contest. Whoever's shell remains unscathed is free to seek out a new opponent. This process continues until only one egg remains unblemished. At which point, the owner of that egg is awarded good luck for the remainder of the year. Logically.

I reach into my pocket and hand Mark a folded sheet of paper. It depicts a dozen exclamation points in a variety of fonts. Mark and I are narrowing down the options for our first tattoos. Only time will tell what demands these exclamation points will make on us in the future. Maybe they'll threaten to cut off all our digits if we don't pick up the bouzouki and master it in six months. Or maybe they'll just put the nail in the coffin to has-been fears . . .

I'm actually writing a new fable. I haven't gotten very far, but I've decided that the protagonist is a moth. I feel like moths are always getting overshadowed by the ostentatious wingspan of butterflies.

So, to help balance the score, I'm trying to write a moral worthy of Mothra. And whether my Aesop rabies peters out afterwards or whether yet a new fable demands to be told is beside the point. Because eruptions happen. What matters is how we irrigate what's erupted.

I ask Mark if being saved by him from the evil clutches of the Sons of Thunder makes me the damsel in distress.

He says, "Killjoy, you're too ugly for that."

"What sucks about being the damsel is that you don't get to pick your hero. I mean, what's to stop some prick from coming along, killing the monster, and taking its place?"

"Ungrateful bitch—"

"Have they started with the eggs?"

"They're just about to. I'll get the azaleas; you get Papou the egg."

I curtsy and run home.

A handful of relatives in the backyard hold paper plates, but little else has changed. There's still the same famished look in their eyes. I open the door and navigate through the hallway in search of Papou. Galloping down the stairs, Dad calls my name. He's holding a charcoal cat in his hands. It's little Zargon, the stray I've been fostering . . .

"One of your cousins opened the door," he says, "and the cat bolted like a laser for the attic."

"Odd . . ."

"Or suspicious?"

I reach in my pocket for a red herring. I pull out a typed version of "The Bear and the Bugle." It's complete with last week's moral.

"What's this?" Dad asks.

"The fable. As promised. And grammatically pure."

Dad hands me Zargon and says, "I'm looking forward to it. I'll try to take a look at it tonight."

"Cool."

He tells me to take the cat out using the front door so that Mom doesn't see. He says, "And get Papou while you're at it."

On Wednesday, I heard Papou practicing with his new

bouzouki. Head bobbing over a binder of sheet-music, he stumbled and fidgeted in the stop-and-go rhythm of practice. I tried my best not to think about the future. I tried to listen in and just let the moment breathe. *Whatever you do*, I said to myself, *don't tug at its string. Put your hands behind your back and let the knot of the present be . . .*

I find Papou outside with two of his great grandnieces in the driveway. Maria is holding a toad cupped in her hands and bringing the amphibian closer to Papou's face. Sophia is huddled behind Papou's wheelchair and peeking out in curious disgust. Eyes closed, lips puckered, the old man is seconds away from kissing the toad.

I let Zargon down and sneak up behind Papou. I say, "*Christos Anesti!*"

Papou breaks free of his spell and lifts up his head. He parrots: "*Christos Anesti!*"

The girls giggle at the old man's sudden excitement.

The words are Greek for "Christ has risen."

I doubt there are two words which Papou enjoys more.

Every Easter, on our way to Norfolk, my parents used to prep me in the car by saying, "Now, as soon as you see Papou, don't forget to say *Christos Anesti*." And being a dutiful grandchild if nothing else, I always screamed out at the top of my lungs as soon as the old man twisted the knob: "*Christos Anesti!*" But it was puzzling to me why Papou got such a kick out of those words. He never seemed like a religious man. In Papou's mishmash mode of storytelling, he was just as likely to add Saint Peter to King Arthur's Round Table as he was to add Odysseus to the Last Supper. But slowly, over the years, I think I've come to understand his enthusiasm for those words. *Christos Anesti*—it's an approval of sorts. An affirmation. An endorsement of how to end all stories. Authors are to leave their audience with an impression that a boulder has been rolled away from a cave and that the air outside has stirred a sepulcher within. It's just easier to say *Christos Anesti* and let the words cast the rest like a shadow of resurrection. Papou, I like to think he came to this conclusion one breezy Easter afternoon. Maybe he opened the front door to the house and was greeted by a great gust of wind—a sneeze from beyond. And maybe he shook his head in response, propped the door open, and said, "You dunderhead, life's not allergic to sepulchers—it's allergic to *all* closed doors!" And maybe he then stepped outside and said, "The self-made wall most of all . . ."

CHAPTER 7

A 17th century galleon scudding the waters of the 8th sea.

Sails the color of Neptune-blue.

Flags the color of Joseph's Amazing Technicolor Dreamcoat.

Cannons loaded with "snakes-in-a-can."

A raven stationed as a lookout in the crow's-nest.

A coyote leaning across the bowsprit.

Falstaff chatting with Hermes under the mizzenmast.

A captain coasting along the deck in a wheelchair, a bouzouki in one hand, a compass in the other.

The direction of that compass: "R." Ruse-ward.

* * *

Fragments of a dream the morning you never woke.